ANNE MARIE WIRTH CAUCHON received her MFA from the University of Montana. She is a PhD student in English, Cultural Studies, and Comparative Literature at the University of Minnesota in Minneapolis. In 2010 she received a MacDowell fellowship for the manuscript of *Nothing*. It is her first novel.

NOTHING
ANNE MARIE WIRTH CAUCHON

TWO DOLLAR RADIO
Books too loud to ignore.

TWO DOLLAR RADIO is a family-run outfit founded in 2005 with the mission to reaffirm the cultural and artistic spirit of the publishing industry.

We aim to do this by presenting bold works of literary merit, each book, individually and collectively, providing a sonic progression that we believe to be too loud to ignore.

Cover photograph: *A tree erupts into flames along Interstate 90 during nighttime burnout operations to keep the Darby Fire from crossing the highway. Montana, Big Timber. 2006 August 30.* NOAA Photo Library
Author photograph: Benjamin Spidahl

Typeset in Garamond, the best font ever.
Printed in the United States of America.

TWO DOLLAR RADIO
Books too loud to ignore.
www.TwoDollarRadio.com
twodollar@TwoDollarRadio.com

ACKNOWLEDGEMENTS

I am especially grateful to the MacDowell Colony, Deirdre McNamer, Eric Obenauf, Emily Pullen, and Eliza Wood, and to my family of friends for their support and assistance. Thank you to my grandmothers, Mary Eleanor Cauchon and Shirley Wirth. Thank you to Janet and Alex Wirth-Cauchon. Thank you, Ben. Thank you, Adaleida.

The strain of holding the I together adheres to the I in all stages; and the temptation to lose it has always been there with the blind determination to maintain it... The dread of losing the self and of abrogating together with the self the barrier between oneself and other life, the fear of death and destruction, is intimately associated with a promise of happiness which threatened civilization in every moment. Its road was that of obedience and labor, over which fulfillment shines forth perpetually.
—Max Horkheimer and Theodor W. Adorno,
Dialectic of Enlightenment

The last to rush past was a woman in a black shawl, carrying the tiny executioner like a larva in her arms. The fallen trees lay flat and reliefless, while those that were still standing, also two-dimensional, with a lateral shading of the trunk to suggest roundness, barely held on with their branches to the ripping mesh of the sky. Everything was coming apart. Everything was falling.
—Vladimir Nabokov, *Invitation to a Beheading*

I see that we meet again.
—Jimi Hendrix to the crowd at Woodstock

NOTHING

ONE

Freak.

I was smoking a cigarette. Bridget was driving, to the party.

She stared at the red light but she was talking about the bum woman in front of the courthouse. Gesticulating at traffic, shouting something I couldn't make out. Bridget hadn't turned to watch the woman, moving like Lou Reed, but she'd seen it all anyway. The skinny black jeans, black jacket, and shades. Everything filthy.

This is why I am *so* out of this town, she said. It's like, a freak magnet. It's like, hell on earth.

I watched my reflection in the side mirror. Truck door, sunglasses, thin arm, blood lips. I let the cigarette drop. It smoked on the street, a long way down. Freak. Lou Reed's mouth moved continuously. She inflated with the flicks of her wrists. Behind her the courthouse clock dwarfed in its steeple. I could end up like that. Like Lou Reed. All it took was one thing after another until you were all the way broken. It was easy; I'd been circling around it forever already. It was nine fifteen but not dark yet. The light went green and Bridget gassed it.

I lit another cigarette.

God, Ruth, how can you smoke in fire season?

I shrugged. She changed lanes, glanced at me from the side of her eye.

Just like breathe.

Bridget was confused when it came to smoking. It was on account of her mom, who spent most days in her brown trailer by the Coke plant smoking Marlboro Lights and watching television. I'd only been there once. But it's not like her mom was fat, she was still hot in that trashy, middle-aged way, and she always had a boyfriend even though she was still in love with Bridget's dad who'd been dead forever. Bridget reached across for my cigarette. The truck swerved and I grabbed for the wheel like an instinct which made Bridget hit me hard in the mouth with the back of her hand. She turned to me lifting the cigarette to her face and took a drag and laughed.

Shit, I'm sorry, she said. But you made the funniest *face*. I didn't really hurt you.

She flicked the cigarette out her window unsmoked. I didn't say anything. For Bridget, I made allowances. I had to. She was my only friend. Which she preferred, having someone on her side exclusively. That was part of the explanation for us, but there were other things, like laws of physics that kept me cuffed to Bridget no matter how much I hated her. For example, we're both good-looking, not rich girls but we have style, and it made us stand out, made us spot each other right off. The first time I saw Bridget I knew right away we'd be best friends. Or enemies.

I leaned back against the steel window frame to watch the hills north of town waver alongside the road, the line between them and the sky blurring where the light got strongest. Bridget was right about Missoula. The fire-ring tightening, the air mutating to smoke getting thicker all the time. The best thing to do was get out of this town before you ended up like all the lifers, crazy or dead. But the thing was, once you were in that was it. From the valley, there's no getting out.

We passed Safeway with its parking lot faded and a couple fat guys waddled through the sliding glass doors with a shopping cart. Behind Safeway was the mountain, as the skiers call it. The mountain was walled in on three sides so all winter the snow fell like light-splinters of the sky whereas the inversion made the valley smoggy, gray, and dry without snow. Because it was walled in, the mountain felt private or like a secret even though there were always a lot of people there skiing, drinking, jumping off shit. But the valley was flat and broad and everything was revealed, nothing hidden, and yet everyone kept pretending there was something left to discover.

Stay like that; I'm gonna take your picture.

Bridget got out her phone. She said, Okay now smile, and glanced up from the little screen. Oh come on, Ruth, it's not hard.

I looked at her.

Fine. Too cool?

There was a pause. I waited. The digitized click.

God you look like… Abraham Lincoln. Tough shit I'm posting it.

Wait okay. Take one more.

I dragged my hair from one side to the other, strained my eyebrows, pointed my face kind of down to avoid a double chin, and smiled like I'd practiced—just enough so everyone I used to know would think things were cool, but not enough to make my face look fat. People always say it's your eyes that betray you when you're lying. I hadn't slept in days; I kept my sunglasses on.

Cute. When you just like try you're totally cute.

Whatever, I said.

And looked to see if she was serious. She handed me the phone. Behind us, a Corolla honked. We both glanced at the rear-view. They must've started designing cars to look like that. Sinister.

Okay take me, she said.

I looked at the photo. I looked good without my eyes. I pointed the phone at Bridget and she shook her bleached head and pretended not to pose. Bridget was a fanatic for her own image with hundreds of self portraits saved into her phone. I scrolled through them, squinting at the little screen. The smoke burned my eyes, the engine and dry wind drowned the synthesizer on the radio so I turned the volume up. The song was *Alberto Balsalm*, Aphex Twin. It's a sad song, with the sound of somebody beating the steel bars of his jail cell. And the synth is melancholic, a little sappy even, but Bridget liked it.

She whispered under her breath.

What? I said.

I didn't say anything, she said and laughed.

Bridget wore skin-tight gray denim cigarette pants and a silk tank. She was gorgeous. She'd bleached her hair a couple weeks ago, a Marilyn Monroe look, and it curled just over her shoulders. Her mouth and eyes were always shining and dry and her breasts were there, her waist and feet were tiny, but that wasn't it, that didn't quite explain it. What explained it was the curse. The curse of the unreasonably pretty, the curse of cult leaders and dictators. It sucked everyone to her, it consumed her, made her untouchable. But Bridget wasn't really cut out for isolation, Bridget was an extrovert, she wanted approval. And partly she got it, walking around with her chin up while every motherfucker got a good look at her face, at her legs, at her ass, but wouldn't talk to her, wouldn't even say hello. Even the girls wouldn't say hello. Except for me.

Whereas I didn't want people to like me exactly. All I wanted was a way out. That's all I'd ever wanted. Even back in Minneapolis suicide was the only thing I could come up with. After that I'd been stupid enough to think I'd found an out in Montana. But then there I was, broke and alone just like before until I met Bridget. That's when I realized all that would happen is I'd forget I ever thought there was some secret in me.

Behind her, to the southwest, a faintly red glow seeped from behind the Bitterroots and through the wettish haze pooling in the valley. The glow sharpened to a point and broke the windshield, making us squint.

God, she said. I wish it were dark already.

We were driving straight west then, and she flipped the visor down. The sun was really burning the cab and her cheeks flushed. She shook her hair off her shoulders and tilted her head back to try and keep the light out. I opened the back windows and turned the volume all the way down. Bridget couldn't stand silence for long, and she started telling a story about some fight she and Lydia had years ago. If I'd been cruel I'd have asked if Lydia would waste her time obsessing about it now, years later, if Lydia would even still remember the stupid fight. But it was a story I'd heard a million times before, and it was easier not to listen.

Outside the truck the fires were spreading. It was in the local paper every day. Even back East the Boston news, and the New York City news covered some of it. There'd been fires around LA and past Phoenix since May or April, seemed like. Then Eastern Washington went, the dead stretch between Idaho Militia Country and Seattle. But it was Montana now too. First it was east, grassfires swelling fast in little nowheres past Billings. Then a little closer, around Yellowstone on the Wyoming side, and after that outside of Ennis, and north of there, by Belgrade. There'd been a picture from the first day all the roads in the park were opened for summer, of the RVs and SUVs and Harleys stopped as if it was rush-hour halfway to the suburbs, with fifty bison in the road, part of the last wild herd, the smoke so thick you had to squint to see the swarm of tourists leaning out of their vehicles, staring into their cellphone cameras in the air. Then southwest of Missoula went, past Darby way back in the River of No Return Wilderness. Bridget said Missoula almost never burned, but when the news came on the TVs over the bar at Charlie B's, the old-timers just shook their heads.

You couldn't see any actual fires from town yet, just a shit-tinged, yellowish haze that crept from behind the mountains every few days and engulfed the sun. At first it would disintegrate by afternoon, and the air in the valley would clear to expose the high-country sun, which burned your skin and sucked the damp from the grasses, and the earth. But the smoke was thickening, breeding, and it lingered, so even on the scorched, sunburnt days the smell hung on.

Today was all right, but hazy, which made it difficult to really *see* what you were looking at, the Sapphires and the Bitterroots and Blue Mountain collapsing in on us. Me silent, and Bridget talking, talking. I couldn't see the mountains clearly like when the air was good, but still at that speed I could feel how the land wouldn't keep a distance. It fell in, then fused with space and spread, rushed from under the truck for the horizon and up. Up. Up to the cumulus and cirrus hung like bodies. The sky cracked open, light seeped out, and it all shoved me down, drew me back up. Up. So that now I evaporated through the roof leaving Bridget forever talking to herself about nothing.

TWO

I was waiting for the train a ways past Craven, South Dakota. And I remembered this pretty girl who gave me a cigarette, leaning on the bumper of her boyfriend's truck. I could tell she liked me, her boots all covered in dust. Now I was looking at the flat horizon, walking in the ditch by the tracks eating bananas. I'd dribble a little Tabasco on, take a bite. The peels I tossed. The bananas I got from a dumpster behind this convenience store and their skin was mostly brown. South Dakota. As far as food I hadn't found much besides bananas. There'd been a Wal-Mart in Sioux Falls. But they poured bleach all over everything. Bleach all over the strawberries. Bleach all over the cupcakes, the pepperoni. Couldn't eat any of it. Not a single person in the whole fucking world could ever eat any of it. That was typical. But it wasn't worth getting worked up over every little thing like that. Because what could I do about it? Nothing.

I sat down on the embankment with the sky everywhere and rolled a cigarette. Lit it and looked for the train. Should've come by now. All you can do is wait. I got the rail schedule out. Should've left Aberdeen, been through this shithole already. I walked back toward town, kicking at the rocks, hands in my pockets. Thinking Montana, thinking nothing, thinking how I might've looked if this scene was a movie.

Everywhere flat and then I heard it. Low, long whistle. Shit. I crouched in the grass, stood up again. Made sure my boots were laced, yanked my pack straps tight, watched its pig nose pointing at me. Watched it pick up speed, spat. Shit. I could've stuck close to town, where it's still slow. I should've talked to the old hobos wavering by the Saloon, for tips, for information. But I'd kept my distance. First three rules: you could die, you could die, don't get caught. It's not like I was afraid. I mean, anymore they've got FBI watching for the likes of me—transients, hitchers. Which was cool, it was hardcore. But if I'd gone out too far from town and the train had picked up so fast I couldn't keep up long enough to jump I'd be stuck another day. Or dead.

You could die, you could die, don't get caught.

Then it was already happening, like always. The train blocked the light all rusted steel and was on me. Huge shrieking tearing fucking drum kit that train. Iron wheels on iron tracks, steel hitches on steel hooks. I lay flat in the grass. So the conductor wouldn't see, but the lonely bastard could use the company. I stood up in its shadow and ran.

Its wake thick with rubberish smoke and air because a train grabs the air by the balls. A train makes its own fucking air. And this one's stank like diesel and burning metal on metal. Mess of skater tags and gang tags on the cars passing was the only living thing but me. And I ran. I ran looking back over my pack to scan the cars all covered in tags coming and passing. I ran scanning the cars passing for a way on up.

Three open-air flatbeds at a distance. The first came quick and I grabbed a rail on it and ran. Fumbling with my left hand that rail cold as hell and rough with rust and sharp. Sliced my squishy palm but I fucking ran. My strides stretched and stretched all like Achilles like I'd take off and fly but I couldn't see a way on up. Couldn't get my right hand situated, couldn't swing my leg up, couldn't see anything but the big flat brown horizon passing. Then I stumbled.

But grabbed on with the fingers of my right hand so I was hanging there by my fucking *fingers* with it picking up speed. I don't know how I swung one foot up on it but I did, hauled my chest up, my ass, rolled to a stop in the middle of the flatbed gasping. My left palm all tore up and bleeding and I grabbed at it but I couldn't feel a thing. Lay gasping and touched my chest to make sure I was all there, but I couldn't feel a thing.

THREE

I can't believe you quit.

I opened my eyes and glanced at her. The Missoula Valley fell away when we rounded the fat corner and the Bitterroot Valley opened modestly before us. Mountains on our right slapping the sky and ground, mountains on our left hunched, beat down. The small ranches wide and green in between, the river, the rail, the bison, black clumps scattered across their grassy cage. Before I quit I bought these motorcycle boots, and I spent some time staring at them, picturing how I must look. I'd wanted to quit for so long. Until this summer, I didn't hate it anymore. Waiting had broken me. And so I quit, because if I didn't care it meant that what I had left was almost gone. But it took that last little bit to actually do it, and now I was nothing. I wasn't paying attention, I'd dropped ash on the edge of my skirt. But when I rubbed it just transformed into a white smear.

You *need* that job, don't you?

I don't know.

I gave up rubbing and looked at my new boots. I wore a gray-green tank top, a denim mini, and I didn't have a purse. I had Christian Dior lipstick in my back pocket, my phone, and four hundred dollars in cash. That's what I had left after paying for the booze and whatever else. I'd been working my ass off for months, all summer so far, and that's all I'd been able to save. It was a fucking joke. As long as I was in school, my dad would keep sending checks. Which meant I'd have to start going to class again, in the fall. Not that he'd find out if I didn't. Anyway, those checks weren't enough to live on really. So I'd have to come up with something, sooner or later. I took a drag and tried to remember what I used to say about waiting tables, before things had changed, before I felt nothing at all.

What? Bridget said.

It's demoralizing. Like you're not there. Nobody looks you in the eye.

That's called life, Ruth, Bridget said. Nobody gives a shit about anybody.

I looked back out the window.

Anyway, she said. *Everybody* hates their job.

That's life, I thought. *That* is life. I was ready for a drink. I was ready for the party, where Bridget would know everybody and they'd stare, but she'd only talk to me. Her lips close, she'd whisper in my ear. She'd been going since high school. Back then she'd been in with Lydia and Audrey, even though they'd tortured her in elementary school. I guess eventually they'd decided she was all right on account of her looks, and her clothes. Bridget always bought designer clearance, consignment. And made sure they never saw her mom's place, or found out her parents were never married, or how her dad had died. It was Bridget who heard about the parties in the first place, from one of the older guys she knew. She told Lydia and Audrey about it, to impress them, and they decided to sneak out and go.

They were young that first time, fifteen or something, and they were poking around upstairs like it was just a big joke when they heard somebody screaming in the master bedroom. So they ran down the stairs, all set to leave but when they made it to the bottom some older guys were waiting, and asked them if they wanted to have some fun. Bridget didn't remember what happened after that, but she'd gotten an invitation ever since. The other thing Bridget didn't remember was why those girls quit talking to her. Or that's what she told me.

I guess they're just shallow, she'd said. Or jealous.

It'd always been so obvious she was lying.

I got the invitation out of the glove box. The hosts weren't too organized, always getting them out last minute. Unless they did it on purpose, which was possible. This one was printed on expensive linen paper and it said, Please arrive no later than ten, casual attire, in small textured black print and that was all. I looked at it as if some other message might appear but it didn't.

FOUR

Took me two days, three trains, and one More-smoking asshole who picked me up hitching just past Butte but didn't have the courtesy to wake me when we rolled through Missoula to find myself fifty miles past my destination. But I did not once think, I've got the cash, I'll catch the next Greyhound. I had to conserve funds. Plus the Greyhound was for sorry sons of bitches, for welfare leeches. Whereas hitching was hardcore, it was my free choice. So although I could have been pissed, when I woke up with this mess of wild peaks in front of my eyes and the asshole behind the wheel saying End of the Line like a real comedian, I wasn't.

I hadn't noticed the smoke yet.

So he stopped his Buick on the corner of the rail and the highway between a hunting-fishing outfitter and a mechanic and I stepped out. Flipped him the double birdie just to set the cosmic precedent that I am not to be fucked with. And what do you know he flipped one back and took off burning rubber. That made me smile even though the smoke hit, made my eyes water, and I'd have to find a ride back up the way I'd just come. Even though my hand hurt like hell and I had to shit. Because what all that meant was I needed a drink and what do you know, he'd dropped me across from some brewery called Bitter Root.

At the bar sat some big-hatted trucker-types drinking from mugs with their names on. Jack. Jim. Bud. They gave me a long, cool stare when I came in like they didn't care for the looks of me but they kept their mouths shut. Behind the bar the old beer maid had her back turned. I headed straight for the john. Before I got on the road I wound up telling my mom where I was headed, and she said that was one thing my pops loved about Montana—people mind their business.

In the john I dropped my pack. I didn't know what to do first so I stood grinning at myself in the mirror. Black rail soot across my face, cracked around my mouth. Made my tongue too red, my teeth yellowish like a wolf. Stank like a urinal cake and shit in there but I was in the stall with my pants around my ankles, quick as you please. I came out with my shirt off. Bud at the urinal with his dick in his hand.

You wanna drink you keep your shirt on, he says.

Just washing my hands is all.

Don't need your shirt off to wash your hands, says Bud to his dick.

He zipped his fly and started out the door without washing. Yessir.

I was polite as hell. The filth from me swirled in the sink. I leaned down to roughly wash my face and neck with the bar of soap and brush my teeth. Got a clean shirt from my pack, wiped the soap dry with a paper towel and was back at the bar. The old boys stared me down not saying anything. Didn't seem much like they were minding their business. Seemed to me they were pretty worried about mine. Not like I was scared, not like I gave a shit what they thought of me or didn't. The old beer maid passed me a pale ale and didn't so much as look at me, like I was same as the rest.

Don't get too many of your kind this far down valley, says Bud, mean.

How's that? I said and swallowed.

Drifters, says Bud. Antisocials. Mostly ya'll stick to Missoula.

Glad to hear it, I say. That's where I'm headed.

Figures, says Bud.

He turned back to the bar. Jack and Jim nodded. Slow.

That was it for conversation and they didn't look back at me. I read the names on the mugs hanging upside down behind the bar. Ordered another. Jim did. Then Bud. I was at the bottom of that pour when these two cute hippie girls pushed through the door with rhinestones in the corners of their eyes. One had dreadlocks, not cute like the other who was sallow, mean-eyed. She had a charm anklet that made a lot of noise when she walked. They both ordered barley wine and from where we sat at the bar you could just about see their tits from the sides of their tank tops. I wasn't the only one looking either. Jim was, his eyes slits, working his tongue over the fronts of his teeth real slow.

The one with the anklet stayed behind to pay. Her purplish

hair made her look translucent. The rhinestones at her eyes like bloody teardrops. I smiled at her and she smiled at her wallet. I tried to think of the last time I got laid. Minneapolis, West Bank, Salvage party at The Mansion. Pretty little anarchist brightly tattooed head to toe like a parrot but everybody called her Wren. And that'd been three months ago. I'd been busy since. Setting things straight with my mom, getting the real story about who my father was anyway, if it wasn't Richard. And setting things straight with Richard, with Richard and his money. It'd been so easy to steal, I don't know why I hadn't done it sooner. Guess it took the truth for me to do something drastic, even though I'd known it in my gut all the time.

Richard wasn't my father. Couldn't be.

After I found out for sure, Richard said it was because my mom got pregnant with me that she and my pops finally split for good. On account of me, not even born yet, that he'd been blind drunk for days, and started the fire that killed him. Let me tell you that is some heavy shit to lay on a person. And it's not like I'd given Richard such a hard time. Because I admit it, in high school, the party people didn't think much of me, and I didn't think much of anybody else. So there I'd be, listening to some old screamcore on my headphones, and here Richard'd come tap-tapping on my shut door to say, Wasn't I doing something with my friends tonight? To which I would say a.) Don't have any or b.) Nothing. He'd have liked it better if I'd been caught up in drugs, in boozing, if I'd got my ass in rehab, something.

I kept living at home while I was going to the CC. That's when it all got worse. He'd get on me like, You've got to *do* something, *be* somebody. And I'd say, Like what? Like who? Tell me, I'd say. I'm listening. Tell me something, anything. But Richard, he'd just get mad as hell when I talked like that, when I begged. There must've been so many times he could've said, I'm not your daddy, loser, I'm not your daddy. But couldn't bring himself to do it.

Funny thing is, I meant it, I wanted an *answer*.

But the only answer I got to Be what? Be who? was: Nothing.

Not like I should've gone to Richard for answers. Since he is Mister Self-Sufficiency. As in, the man doesn't believe in banks. So he had, I don't know, three million in bills and gold bars locked in his safe in the basement. I kid you not, Dick was loaded. Which is why what I took from him—ten thousand—is like small potatoes, a drop in the bucket. He might not even notice it's gone. If it wasn't for the gun. A Smith and Wesson 32-20, which is rare for a pistol. The Preacher's Gun, he called it. His pride and fucking joy, he loved that thing so much he'd only shown it to me a couple times and even then he didn't let me touch it. But now it was mine.

Nice night, I said.

The redhead gave the beer maid a fifty. Her wallet was filled with cash.

Not too smoky, she said. You going to the party?

North of here?

Missoula was north. But the girl laughed like I'd said north as a joke.

Yeah. North.

Like it was obvious.

Would be, I lied. But my ride fell through.

She smiled blankly for something to do. Her pupils were huge and she wasn't so cute as I'd thought. I tried to guess what she was on. Acid, molly, amphetamines. Girls like that love to mix their highs. She took her drink over to her friend who didn't look up from her phone, blue light reflecting off the tip of her nose. Hippies.

There was a newspaper at the end of the bar, yesterday's, the front page a belch of black smoke, a tiny figure at the bottom in front, gas-masked, one mini-arm raised, flames. It was the picture that caught my eye. Mostly stories about the fires. One way southeast, by someplace called Aladdin. The smoke so thick and fast-moving that it'd followed the Livingston Brothers and the rest of the biker gangs all the way to Sturgis. Another fresh fire near here, someplace called the River of No Return. I drank, ordered a hamburger.

Sure thing, hon, said the beer maid.

The skin around her eyes was blackish and it sagged, but she forced a smile. Nobody likes a sad waitress. The redhead leaned in.

If you're ready you can come with us.

The beer maid put the burger on the bar. She had on a flashy wedding ring studded with cheap blood diamonds. The burger was in this little red basket. She sighed.

Burger, she said.

The redhead didn't wait for a reply, turned. But I couldn't move and just sat there all frozen like there had to be a catch. She pushed through the door with her bony hip. Her friend must've been outside already. But this was my ride, I was thinking, this was what I needed, a way back toward Missoula, no waiting. It couldn't be easier, this had to be it. Plus I'd made myself a deal at the start, take what comes, like I imagined my pops would've done. And these hippie girls were what'd come. I drained my beer and looked in the mug. Put a twenty on the bar and looked at that. Smiled at the beer maid. Slow. Nodded to the old boys who didn't look. But then I stood up, took my burger basket in hand, swung on my pack and was back outside where my eyes stung and watered, something like dry snow fell from the sky and it smelled like wildfire.

The girls stood by this old blue Ford F-250 crew cab with the doors open and the Dead Bears on the bumper. Some ride for a hippie. On the back seat they had a filthy car seat but I couldn't see if there was a kid in it. If there was, neither of them was paying it any mind. Then a puny hand with tiny filthy fingernails grabbed at the edge of the seat, then at the air and disappeared. Maybe I heard it whimper, but that didn't mean anything to me.

I walked around to the back of the bed and grabbed open the tail's handle, which fell with a clank. I'd been in the wind for forever already but I had a good beer buzz going, and the burger, so I figured I could hack it in the back of the truck. The bed was empty except for a case of champagne and a case of gin.

You don't mind riding in back, right?

That was the one with the dreads. You could tell she'd only grown the dreads to try and get mommy's and daddy's attention. Only she didn't know how to care for them right and they'd turned nasty. I wasn't into that hippie bullshit, but sometimes you've got to do something to break out, anything, pick something that'll piss your folks off and go with it. Which I guess had meant pissing off the evil stepdad, Richard. I grinned. It felt great to say, Richard the evil stepdad. And I felt all right in the truck bed, like a natural, like it was in my blood. Maybe this was what my pops would've done, had done, leaned in a truck bed just like this and looked up at those shapely old mountains feeling just like me.

FIVE

Bridget's truck dipped, going the wrong way over the wheel ruts up to the door of the party house. It had been built at the peak of the housing boom but never lived in. Stupid beige house ridiculous under the Bitterroots that fractured like stone fingers finger-fucking heaven. It stood by itself in the grasses and flat land, at the mouth of Bear Canyon. You've seen this house a million times before: beige vinyl siding, sparsely scattered tiny cheap windows and one picture window in the living room that doesn't open, a faux turret covered in lick-and-stick brick, shellacked oak doors with gleaming brass handles. To its right a rotting barn collapsed and five sprinklers misted the wheat in loose arcs. Horses flicked their tails at the flies and bent their heads before the cliffs. There were only a few cars so far, two pick-ups—three including Bridget's—a Subaru, and a Hummer I'd never seen. The Hummer was black, with dealer plates from Mack's Used Automotives in Louisville, Kentucky.

But inside, things were different since it was mostly gutted, all the carpet and most of the walls on the first floor ripped out to make a room big as a warehouse. They'd ripped the wallpaper off the exterior walls so they were smeared with dirt-coated glue and with red graffiti that said things like, I die. Or like, No outside, Nothing but outside.

I checked my eyeliner in the visor mirror and pictured myself with a drink. Tonight would be like always, everybody'd get glassy-eyed and mean, and leer at the randoms and the boys would fight. Except for the Forest Service helicopters overhead toting water tanks down valley to the River of No Return fire, it sounded like any party. That and last time, a kid nobody knew, a kid who said he was just passing through from Portland, found Drew Stone in the grass about a half-mile from the house, beat to shit, missing teeth, unconscious. When he woke up in the hospital, he said he didn't remember a thing. At least to the doctors. But we all knew he was lying.

We didn't need to knock since the cheap double doors were off their hinges and leaned against the vinyl siding. We stood in the doorway with bottles of bourbon and bottles of champagne in our arms and scanned the room. Everybody was supposed to bring champagne. Red curtains covered the windows, so the place had that creepy bloody look like a darkroom. Some sedated music played from speakers stacked in the corners and the long, low velveteen couches were pushed back against the walls. It smelled like lemon cleaner, cigarette smoke, and liquor.

On the yellow couch just right of the door, the couch where Bridget and I always sat, were some plain-faced girls with natural tans and muscular legs, and they looked up at us trying to mask their confusion. They didn't know what they were supposed to be doing, but they knew this was a *party*, and if they ever wanted to come back, they'd better go with it. One had braces. One was abnormally small, the runt. You could tell they recognized Bridget, they gave her the once-over.

Haven't seen those girls since *high school*.

They stole our seats, I said.

Then, I saw them. Across the room on the red sofa sat Lydia and Audrey. Bridget switched a champagne bottle from one hand to the other and cleared her throat. They were always at the parties, but were usually last to arrive since everyone's invitations were different. That made it easy for Bridget to ignore them. Or for them to ignore her. Audrey lay against one arm of the sofa with her eyes closed, her hair all wild. Lydia was reading a magazine and slowly bouncing this totally perfect yellow sandal.

Think they're driving the Hummer? I whispered. I meant it like a joke.

What? We started across the room, Bridget walked slightly in front of me.

The *Hummer*, I said to the back of her head.

We reached the part of the room that had been the kitchen. Bridget looked at me like she wasn't listening so I gave her a phony smile, set the bottles on the counter and started to fix myself a drink. Bridget was standing too close, which I didn't like much.

Neither of those girls drives a Hummer, she whispered. Lydia drives, oh what's it called? Expedition? Liberty?

There was a DJ in a caged stage mounted on the far wall. He was a skinny kid with a face like a rat. A girl in a metallic blue mini holding a camera sat very upright next to him with her ankles crossed. She was rubbing her nose. The music was languid and loose and smoky. The beat sounded like it was pounded into a piece of brass. There was a saxophone but no words.

Bridget glanced at Lydia and Audrey across the room and laughed. Something was up, something was different than normal, and she was nervous.

You *know*? she said.

Totally, I said.

It was good, us together. Like a team or something. So maybe things would turn out all right, I thought. I uncorked one of the champagne bottles and poured. When I looked up, Lydia stood leaning over the counter watching me.

Hello. She paused. It's Edith, right? She sounded drugged, her voice was thick. She didn't smile.

Hey Lydia. My name's actually Ruth. Like in the Bible? We'd been through this before.

Lydia with severe, gaping dark green eyes. It was uncomfortable staring into them but she didn't blink. She was tall and expectably thin and wore a faint lilac skirt made of torn layers like industrial lace, and a pale sleeveless raw-silk blouse. She smelled prim like cream and honeysuckle, and it didn't suit her.

I'm glad you could make it, Lydia said.

As if this were her party. But nobody knew the hosts, they were supposed to be from out of town. New York by way of Jackson Hole, that's what most people said. And everybody thought they'd met one or the other a couple times, but were too fucked up to remember exactly. Anyway, it meant I knew I couldn't roll my eyes even though she wasn't looking at me. She was looking at Bridget, at her new blond.

Thanks? I said anyway.

Bridget didn't say anything. It was this kind of unspoken agreement we had. When it came to Lydia and Audrey, I'd do the talking. Or that's what I figured.

Lydia looked at Bridget's shoes, then at her cigarette pants, and at her tank top. Then she smiled a little and looked in the vicinity of Bridget's eyes.

It's so good to *see* you, Bridget. Audrey and I were just saying. It's been *forever*.

I know, Bridget said. I was just thinking. It's been forever.

Your hair's cute, Lydia said. Not everybody could pull it off. But you totally look like. Marilyn Monroe or something. I'll tell Audrey you said hello.

I drank quickly and watched her cross the room. Bridget read the back of one of the bottles, biting the inside of one cheek and pretending not to smile. It was so obvious. She'd never said it, but I knew if they took her back, she'd drop me in a second. She sighed and didn't look at me. Filled her glass and drank but didn't look at me.

I'm gonna smoke, I said. I'll be back.

Outside the day faded to dusk and there was little movement but the wind's. There was nobody in sight. Escaping light dyed the sky white. On the other side of the valley the Sapphire Mountains glowed pink with dark green pockets tracing the creek beds. It was places like that the recluses lived. By a creek, off the grid. But the valley stayed between me and the Sapphires with lots of smoke and dust hovering over the swaths of dry grass.

I sighed and went back in, sat down near the end of the yellow couch where the randoms were. It was *our* couch. When Bridget eventually sat I gave her a look like, Hey, but couldn't think of anything to say. It was so obvious she wanted to go sit by Lydia and Audrey but didn't have a good enough excuse. I leaned back, looked up at the ceiling, and the room turned cavernous like a church but nothing happened.

I took out a cigarette but didn't light it.

Give me one, Bridget said.

The girls watched, tucking their hair behind their ears. I held one cigarette softly between my lips and leaned forward, made a flame. When it lit our skin touched. We were the more beautiful.

I thought this would be a comfort to Bridget but it wasn't.

Her eyes flicked across the room, where Audrey curled and uncurled her long fingers and licked her lips. Cream and honeysuckle mixed with the liquor stench and the smoke.

Um, excuse me, said the runt. Do you mind smoking outside? She flapped her hand in front of her face. Bridget gave the girl a look, and exhaled smoke on smoke. The girl's hand dropped into her lap. She wore earth-green outdoors gear: shorts made from a lightweight waterproof material, a cotton t-shirt in an athletic cut, and large, comfortable-looking sandals. Except for her size, she was totally anonymous. Except for the birthmark. A thick maroon pond, it seeped upward and disappeared beneath the shorts.

I can't remember. Have you always had that? Bridget asked the girl, pointing to her leg but looking her in the eye.

I made some kind of noise in protest but right away I wished I hadn't.

What? Bridget said. I'm just curious if she's always had that thing on her leg.

She turned back to the girl whose mouth was open, her teeth small and pointed like a vampire's. Lydia and Audrey watched from across the room.

Is it a birthmark? Or a *scar*.

I felt sorry for the girl. She was probably nice enough. Boring, but nice. I tried smiling at her but she didn't see. Her friend leaned forward and brushed her elbow.

You don't have to say anything, Ruth, the friend said.

Oh. My. God, Bridget said. I completely forgot. Ruth! Her name is Ruth *too*.

While she said it she turned to me with her lips curled, her eyes on fire. She was ferocious, like an animal freshly caught. She glanced across the room. Like Lydia and Audrey were her old masters whom she loathed and loved and who'd just caught her again. There she was groveling, doing her old tricks to impress them, like a dog.

You ladies have the *same name*, Bridget said.

They must've planned it. It must've been a practical joke, a set up. To show me what I really was, from the outside. And if Bridget hadn't been in on it, she was now. Or was trying to be. She turned back to the other Ruth. I didn't feel like trying to smile at her anymore. Across the room Lydia and Audrey were whispering. Up on stage the rat-faced kid held his oversized headphones to his ear and rocked back and forth mechanically. His girl had a sheet of steel on a little table before her and she'd bent over it to blow some lines of coke.

I stubbed out my cigarette on the sole of my sandal and stood up.

Where are you *going*, Ruth?

I gave her a look. Lydia perched on the edge of the sofa examining herself in a compact. Her hair was flat and silken, it stopped just above her waist. Audrey carefully replaced a large ring and straightened her dress. The other guests would arrive soon. At the counter I poured myself another drink.

When the music changed Lydia was the first to dance. She stepped slowly from the sofa, her right hand floating from her body, her light clothes misting about her. Audrey paced before the sofa like a caged young panther before she walked to the middle of the room and laughed. She whispered to Lydia, took a little vial from the red satin coin-purse between her fingers and waved her hand for me to come over. When I got there Bridget was with them already and she wouldn't look at me. Audrey handed me the vial. There wasn't really a choice at the parties, you took what came around. So I got two tiny blue pills on my fingertip and took the flask, which was Bacardi. I handed the vial to Bridget who swallowed them dry.

What are they? the other Ruth said.

She peered inside.

This your first party? Bridget said. Take one. You'll regret it if you don't.

She glanced at Lydia, who smiled.

But what are they?

Party favors, Lydia said. You want to enjoy yourself, don't you?

It's probably just molly.

But it was wishful thinking; I wasn't trying to convince her.

Molly? the other Ruth said.

But she took one anyway. Audrey put the vial back in her purse without taking one herself, without drinking from the flask. This I tried immediately to ignore or forget since it meant nothing good for the rest of us. For a little while we stood around not talking or pretended to dance looking each other over until we were all guilty, until we'd all forgotten who or what we'd done.

SIX

The dreadie gunned the engine as soon as she got it started and spun out of that parking lot, bumped over the tracks. Shit I had to hang on to my burger. But I could do this, it was in my blood, I was a natural. We drove north, the smoke in the air clearing as we drove. On the left were the Bitterroots. Gorgeous, huge, moving. One broke at the top like a castle's spires. One came to a peak like a nipple. Dark canyons between each mountain vacuumed the rolling pastures in toward them so it all disappeared behind the wall of the range. I can't explain it. Tiny horses, tiny ranch houses scattered around in front.

When I finished the burger I tossed the basket at the ditch. Scooted back, and leaned against the truck's slick metal ridges. The girls had some house music on loud. Terrible shit, some kind of raver thing, and the bass rattled the sliding windows. After a little the window slid open and a bottle came out.

Bacardi. Which was typical but I wasn't picky so I stuck the bottle between my knees, unwrapped my hand, took a pull, soused the wound—it was rough and blackish—and winced but didn't yell. The girls were smoking a joint.

Once I got my hand wrapped again I stood up. The big wind pushed me back, made my eyes water. We must've been going ninety. The light faded, turning cool and blue in the center, pale pink on the hills, at the edges. And those fucking mountains like God's pornography or something, but it was dumb to try making comparisons.

Pretty soon we turned onto gravel. The truck bumped over two wheel ruts that led to this ugly beige McMansion with some Harleys and a Hummer, about fifteen vehicles total parked in the dead grass around it. The truck stopped but the girls took forever getting out—checking their rhinestones in the visor mirrors and lighting cigarettes. Finally they let the truck doors swing open and cleared their throats and not looking at each other. They took forever smoking their cigarettes too, so I rolled one and I'd smoked it down by the time they got the champagne and gin from the bed. The dreadie handed me three gins and said something so quiet I couldn't make it out.

The redhead looked up at me from the gin in her arms and smiled a little, her brow all knit. She bent to set the bottles in the grass and unbuckled her sandals. Then buckled them again. The dreadie got the kid out of its car seat but she had a blue blanket over its head so I couldn't see its face. They lit another smoke and stood staring at the house.

I followed the redhead to this kitchen counter that looked like it'd erupted through the floor since there wasn't a kitchen around it. Just a big tore-up room with some red graffiti on the black walls. Girls dancing in the middle of the room, girls sitting around on beat-up velvet couches. I dropped the bottles at the counter.

Make you a drink?

The redhead smiled. I poured us gins on the rocks. She was standing a little close so I stepped back and smiled noncommittal and dapper like, No hard feelings, honey. But she didn't get it. She smiled back, blinking a lot and got close again.

Hey. Hey what's your name anyway?

What? she said.

The voices were loud, the music. Clumps of girls here and there whispering, sipping and watching each other, watching the boys spill from the door and flash invitations and scan the room. High ceilings and the unfinished floor stained with liquor or urine or blood. Graffiti on the walls. Dim reddish indirect lights from above, red cloth across the windows, cigarette smoke and sweet grass smoke or incense. The girls were the only decoration. Frat boys with whiskey stormed in, handed off their invitations without looking and took in the room like they were looking for somebody to fuck.

I said, I hissed into her ear. What's your name?

Sasha, she said. Come on.

She started across the room. I'd forgotten how small a girl's hand could be, how soft and crushable.

The frat boys had already commandeered the middle of the room. And they laughed, swilling from the bottle with a couple mousy girls dancing in front of them like they'd seen on TV. Frat boy got a smoke from his pack, lit it, took three steps up to the one dressed for hiking with this huge red mark on her leg. He got his hand on her ass. She didn't even look back over her shoulder at him, stopped dancing, staggered.

I mean everyone was there—preppies, hippies, squares, the rock kids. But the punks were sparse, which made things a little easier. Meant I didn't have to prove I was for real. Not that there was any question. But you know. We're a tough crowd.

The redhead stopped at a dark stairway I hadn't noticed but didn't let go of my hand. There were these two perfect girls dressed like this was a fashion shoot. Plus a beautiful one with naughty slant eyes and her hair bleached blond like Monroe, and one imperfect, sad one smoking a cigarette. Monroe I recognized. Way out here in Montana, and right off there's some chick I'd seen before. Or thought I'd seen. I kept looking back at her face, at her bleach-blond, at her eyes, at her mouth moving, like I'd seen it all before. I couldn't stop staring, looking back again, again. Her lips apart, her eyes on her friend so I looked too. Déjà vu. Made my head spin but I couldn't place her, couldn't place her. Monroe, Monroe. Maybe I'd seen them both before? But I didn't think so. Her lips, slant eyes, slim and well-built. It was a bad sign. It meant I was done for. It meant I was on a collision course pointed straight at her and her sad little friend since girls like that need each other, use each other.

Monroe.

Or maybe she was just another copy of the standard desperate girl, trying to be like from a magazine. And I could tell just by looking at her that she was bad news. You'd think about it whenever she was out of your sight—all manner of sorry motherfuckers with their eyes on her. You'd stay up nights thinking about it until you were nothing but hating them for wanting her, until you were nothing but hating her, until it all came true.

Ruth, Monroe said. Ruth.

This Ruth stubbed out her cigarette before she turned. So I could get a good look. And she was all right, she was good. The kind who'd do anything you asked, so long as you showed a little tenderness. Her I could get.

They said you should come upstairs too, said the redhead. If you want.

Monroe glanced at the perfect girls, then at me and away. It wasn't her mouth, it was something in her eyes I recognized, and her brows, which were dark. Like her bleached hair was a disguise. Ruth looked at me then too. Straight at me as if I'd said her name aloud. Her I didn't recognize, but still I knew I was right about her. Easy. And she looked good, not like Monroe but good. Murky dark green eyes and a short skirt with something smeared on it. Motorcycle boots, no tattoos, hair dyed black. She stared across the room at the front doors and the night like she was thinking of making a run for it. But when we started up the stairs she was stuck in the middle of the crush.

The upstairs hall was dim with rows of closed doors on either side. I followed the pack left, to the red door at the end that faced us with a light glowing from beneath, all foreboding. When it opened thick, white shisha smoke rolled out. A large room appeared, dimmer than the hall. I held my breath. Two metrosexual-types inside, crisp oxfords, one pinstriped, the other baby blue. Marketing majors. Richard-types, junior Dicks. Didn't expect their kind in these parts. Didn't expect them to let me in.

You can pay, right? one said.

I guess it was good I laughed because they let me in, looking me over, my bad hand wrapped up in some dirty t-shirt. The one by the door had a stack of bills in his hand, it must've been at least a thousand. He waited. I got out my wallet. He glanced down, and tried not to react when he saw how much I had.

How much? I said.

You're new huh, he said. Ninety.

I gave him a crisp hundred.

We don't do change, he said.

Whatever, I said.

So I was in, whatever that meant. The other guy was tending the hookah in the middle of the room with three small couches and three velvet chairs around it. Neither one looked the girls in the eye, made it obvious they'd fucked all of them or some.

Right off the redhead passed me a flask and smiled looking nervous as hell. I drank and passed it back. I'd already forgotten her name. Nobody paid me any mind, didn't even look. Like they were that high or used to randoms. Monroe kept checking her phone, but I could forgive her even that. It was the way she sat or stood I recognized too: defiant, coy. Her sad little friend stood alone rubbing her face hard with the heel of her hand like she was trying to rub her high off. Then she turned to Monroe, the tip of her chin dragging her face down. Her mouth was large and dark and briefly I imagined fucking it.

The two perfect girls moved together like snakes. One—she had black hair and she was the queen—slid to a loveseat. The other—wild-haired—leaned down to whisper something in her ear and they smiled but didn't laugh. Monroe was their groupie, but I could forgive her that too. Especially that. I knew how she felt. Like how I'd agree with every fucking piece of bullshit Joseph would wax on about at the Salvage meetings, just like Eric, just like Great White and every other punk in the room. Autonomy. Black market bartering. Revolt. Racial partitioning. After Harriet showed up and everybody turned on Joseph calling him a skinhead, I turned on him too.

Monroe leaned in to try and hear what the perfect girls were whispering. She faked a knowing smile glancing back at Ruth, who, I realized, saw everything even through her high. I touched her elbow.

She flinched and glanced back at me over her shoulder.

Sorry, I said.

What? she said.

She half-turned, but she wasn't looking at me.

Sorry. Didn't mean to scare you.

What? she said. I'm not *scared*. Why would I be scared?

She walked very carefully to one of the low-slung velvet chairs and sat down staring hard at Monroe who perched herself on the arm of the loveseat since the two didn't make it easy for her to find room on it. For a little while she tried to pretend she liked it there, balancing on the edge. Ruth whispered something under her breath, dropped her head on her hand in surrender. The hookah base was kryptonite and the water in it laughed at the drags. Nobody said a thing.

It was my turn to smoke when the dreadie came in without knocking but with her baby slung over one forearm, three bottles of champagne and cups tucked in the other. The baby's bald head hung, speckled with birthmarks. The girls on the loveseat didn't look up. Downstairs, voices spawned, swelled to a crowd's scream. The dreadie put the baby on the floor where it lay turning its filthy face from side to side, weakly curling and uncurling its body like a worm. From her pocket she took a vial and she made this face. I guess it was a smile.

Perfect timing. Crystal.

The dreadie nodded, pale as her baby. She handed over the vial and sat down. The pretty boy by the hookah poured champagne into the little plastic cups. He wore loafers and his hair was in this wave. He'd bleached his teeth, or they were false. Which I heard was common among the one-percent. The redhead passed me a plastic cup and everyone drank. It was quiet but for heaving breathing on the edge of the plastic and this funny sucking sound with fizz. The dreadie kept her eyes on the vial.

The marketing major at the door had the collar of his blue polo popped.

There's a baby on the floor, he said. What, is it a joke?

I wish, the dreadie said but didn't look.

He stepped from the wall and picked it up gingerly under the arms. Its head fell back but it pulled upright again, the whites of its eyes yellowish, the irises filled with dark nothing. The marketing major held it at arm's length and cocked his head to one side and he said, Aw. It's cute.

No it's not, said the queen. It's like. Totally ugly.

The marketing major laughed. The one with the wild hair took a pill from the vial and passed it. The bottle of champagne was about half-full and I drained it.

That was rude, said the queen.

I licked my lips and put the bottle back on the floor. Carefully. Upright.

I'm not the one who called the kid ugly, I said.

Everybody laughed, except Ruth. But the response was delayed, they were laughing at the queen's joke, not mine.

That was rude, said Ruth. To call a pathetic thing ugly, Lydia. *That* is rude.

It took me off-guard, and I laughed once. I'd have pegged her for one with less balls than that. But she wasn't looking at anybody, she was talking to her drink.

The queen, I guess her name was Lydia, turned in a single, mechanical motion. I don't remember talking to you. She was probably always vicious.

Ruth looked in her direction, but like the baby, she couldn't focus her eyes. This your party? Ruth said. Just tell me. Is this. Your. Party?

Monroe looked between the queen and Ruth without moving her head and laughed in a couple of frightened, pretty chortles, reaching for the baby whose legs feebly bicycled, searching for something to push off against when there was nothing.

Let me see it, Monroe said. Ugh, it smells. Somebody take it, somebody take it!

No no hold it like that. Let me put the hood on it. That was the one with the wild hair.

The vial had come back around to the dreadie. I sat on the edge of our couch, tapping my empty cup on my knee. The red-head lightly rubbed my back like she was my girlfriend but she wasn't. I looked back at her and cleared my throat and shifted away but she kept it up. There was too much happening in the room, between all these thick, attractive people. I had to get out of there. This was my first night in Montana. This was supposed to be a party, and here I was watching some girl's good-as-dead baby loll its stupid head on its puny neck. What a joke, I was thinking. What I needed was to get downstairs, where the music was, where the liquor was, and dance.

SEVEN

Kid in the cage said, *Nuttin Like Assassination Day*, and played it. I'd danced forever, licked my cracked lips, still had my drink. Brought it down from overhead and tipped the rim and lapped for water but there was none. Gasped. Breathing suffocated and I gasped. The smell was putrid, soured, sickly sweet like the Secret, the Edge, the One. Human skin slick with sweat smeared against me as shoulders surrounded me. And throats and hair. There weren't any human eyes but there was the music.

Kid in the cage said, *Under the Influence*, and played it. I dropped the cup I had. I couldn't see the floor. My knees danced down. Down but I couldn't see the floor. Under the influence. I checked my pockets for the cash. What the fuck you mean can't see the floor? A private joke, Ruth says hands on her head Ruth says hands on her ass hands on her tits ha ha. I took a step as if this was dancing.

Kid in the cage said, *Indo Silver Club*, and played it. So I got it, I had it, I could fucking dance; I could dance forever. I lifted my body. I shook my rib. Cage. And chin. With a throat so loose I'd better shut my eyes. Hands like untamed pigeons flew. If there was an above the heads for real, I'd have flew too.

Kid in the cage said, *Protect Ya Neck*, and played it. I got one open wandering eye alight on Ruth's scar. Which spread and spread, ran and hid up under the good shorts. Comfortable shorts. Practical. Splotch pulsed, its own body. Whatever you do, do not look. My nothing but slit eyes drug dragged across her hips and arms. Watch your step kid. Watch your step kid.

She pumped her pelvis off beat and licked her lips with a little tongue, eyes half-shut. Like mine I'd imagine. So I was all, You've got to get her the hell out of here out of here here, you get her out here.

So I looked above us for where there'd be no shoulders throats or scars, for where there'd be no body, for a scrap of clear air free air but above they just had smoke. Like outside. Kid in the caged rocked his torso non-stop. His blue metallic dress paced, photographing between the bars. Long lens zoom copy record. Somebody's always watching. Watching me, watching that Ruth's scar throb. Which is my name. Which is what they say I am called. I hid my face but when I said Stop the sound was lost. Then. There was a voice I'd heard before.

What have you done, it hissed.

And stopped. A woman's voice.

What did you do, it said. What did you do? God. God. What did you do?

Like that, just like that. My hands dropped from my head to my hips and I stood still and looked. Everywhere was lips. Then the voice. And it all began again. I couldn't make the words out. It could've been Bridget. She'd been dancing close by. I brought my head around to see, and there she was. Bridget blond as hell but she just stumbled head loose, eyes blind like she couldn't talk and hadn't.

A soft light came.

Kid in the cage said, *Contract on Love*, and played it. Which started with clapping then Wonder sang, baby baby sign right here on this dotted line and you'll be mine till the end of time. I mouthed the words. In a wave dancers' faces turned and they lifted up their cellphones! The little blue lights, the blue lights washed back and lit us from above. A hollow was made for Lydia and Audrey to step up and dance. Like always I looked back at Bridget. She swayed but she was looking right at them, she *saw* them. She always saw them, she was always seeing them in her mind's eye. Shoulders and torsos swarmed me. I was struck in the face and inhaled my own bone smell and blood smell with iron and thick.

Let me out, I tried to yell. Goddamn let me out.

I'd said it aloud since a man, black-haired, mean-browed, leaned over me. So I'd collapse in his arms like a fresh corpse, so I'd beat him off with my bony fists until he was through. If he grabbed my wrist, I'd never escape. I stared up at him. The Evil Eye tattooed behind his ear. Watching me. This was it. Let me go, I hoped I'd said aloud. This was the end. He had me by the arms. His face breeched, wet red cavity yawned and the teeth, teeth. I gasped.

Hey, he said. Hey. Hey.

I stared up at his eyes, I'd seen him before, his hair damp with sweat and stuck to the weak skin circling his ears, the Evil Eye. Evil Eye. I reached for Bridget but she didn't see, *her* eyes were glass, her arms in the air. She shook, dancing with her head loose. I tried to pull away but there was nowhere to go and he had me by the arm, he had me by the small of my back. His grip was stiff, I buckled in pain and tried to sit but couldn't. He yanked me to slouch standing. He had Bridget by the wrist.

Hey, he said. Relax, all right? You *want* out?

EIGHT

Shit, he said outside.

The fire stink hung in the thin air. Bridget took two steps along the wall and sat hard in the dust. I tossed him off and tried to run but didn't make it far.

It's not like I'm going to try and fuck you, he said.

I stopped and crouched and leaned over my knees with my

head down. Dawn was close. I flicked my head up and leaned back against the wall and watched him but he was rolling a cigarette, he didn't look my way. Which made me think I needed a smoke, before daybreak encased me. I got one whole out of my crushed pack and lit it. I tried to count my cash but my hands shook. Looked like two hundred. I couldn't remember spending that much. I looked the man over, but he just smoked his flaccid little rollie and didn't raise his eyes, didn't make a move. His other hand he had wrapped up in some filthy makeshift bandage. I could ask about it. For something to say.

Dawn could come, anytime. I looked for a crust of White Light on the tip of a mountain or on the horizon but didn't see any sign of sunrise. I leaned against the wall. I wanted this fucking night done. The vinyl siding cut into my backstraps. I sat on my heels and traced my finger on the ground.

Thanks, I said. Things got a little confused. I didn't know if...

Confused? he said. What *was* that?

Bridget slumped down the wall and quietly vomited into the dust.

Like her, he said. Extreme turnoff.

What, I paused. Bridget?

I wrote Dawn with my finger in the dust.

And upstairs I was like, total babe, he said. Shit. I mean just look at her.

But I didn't. I brushed Dawn away and looked at my dirty fingers, looked at the edge of the sky, where the sun would come. Maybe the black was turning bluish in the faint first light. Maybe I felt a little better. But all that was going to happen was the smoke would settle in thick again. I shook my head and did look at Bridget, who mewed, making soft little sounds, her head hanging over the gray puddle of vomit.

You okay, Bridget?

I swear I recognize you, he said through a grin.

Don't lie, I said.

What? He shrugged, all innocence. I'm not lying.

His fake smile, dapper and lewd.

I've never seen you in my life, I said.

He decided not to let his gaze respond. But he stared for too long.

Fine, he said. Fine you're right.

And pointed hard at Bridget, like he hated her. It was always that way with the parties, bodiless rage that materialized haphazardly, without cause. Or the result became the cause. Like this: him with his accusation-finger upheld. He pulled on the butt of his rollie and snubbed out the puny cherry between his black thumb and finger. The tobacco he scattered around. The scrap of paper caught the wind, and there was nothing left.

It's *her* I recognize, he said. Your friend or whatever.

Which infuriated me unreasonably. For her. But for me more. She's heard that *before*, I said. She hears that shit all the time, man.

He stubbed out his cigarette watching Bridget. Now I couldn't tell if it was loathing or lust, or if he thought watching her was something he needed to survive. Bridget pretended to be dead, her head hanging, her arms limp. She looked like shit but he didn't care. So they deserved each other, I thought, looking up at him from the ground, from at his feet where I slouched. I hated them both. Just a couple of fucking clichés, play-acting at being themselves. He turned his slant eyes and dark brows back to me and paused, seeing past me, through me like I wasn't there.

She's drunk, I said. We took some molly before the party started and.

That wasn't molly, he said. Just look at her. *I'm* drunk. But her?

He walked toward me with his palm poised at Bridget, blessing her. Shadows filled his eye sockets, darkened where his gaze fell.

And who are you? I said. I don't know you. Who are you anyway? I don't even know. Who you are.

He stood over me, my head in my hands, my hair in my hands. I would rip it out if he got any closer I would rip it out. My guts filling the esophagus to choke me. Or I would choke me, hair in my hands I'd pull it out and my skull would be there. He and she would laugh. At the blood. Laughter in the blood. Ha ha ha ha.

You're not making any sense, he said, still innocence. You make no sense.

The way he said it: disgusted at me. The way he sucked the thoughts from me. He rubbed his hair, swayed, hands in his pockets, eyes narrowed. It was true I was shit, I'd be lucky to be trash in the orbit of him and her. And yet. He stood over me, wouldn't leave me alone, wouldn't leave me alone. I would cry, I thought. Finally I'd cry.

Fuck you, I said. I don't know you. I stood up. I could stand up.

Fine, he said. Guess I was wrong about you.

Fuck you, I said and shrugged him off even if he wasn't there.

Guess I shouldn't have gotten you off the floor, he said. Guess you're just like them. Like every other sorry motherfucker.

I didn't have anything to say to him, the nobody. I started to walk, keeping my hand on the siding slats, gathering dust on my palm and fingers. I drew my hand away but couldn't stand up like that. If I could just get around the corner and breathe. His breath hot on my neck, I turned over my shoulder to look. If I could just get away from him for a minute and think. He stood behind me, over me, his breath, his stare. I was at the corner, I grabbed the corner and pulled myself to the other side.

But when I opened my eyes I wasn't alone. People loitered there. Boys mostly, and the other Ruth with her shirt off, passed out with her head cocked and her mouth open. I wasn't surprised, nothing could surprise me anymore. She had her left hand out resting on the palm like she was pointing. There was something next to her on the ground. The boys stood doing nothing, drinking from red plastic cups.

Where's your shirt? I said. Ruth. Where is it? Ruth.

But she couldn't hear. I reminded myself this wasn't my problem, but I scanned the ground for her shirt anyway. That's when I saw. It was a baby next to her, a puny monster in the dust. Maybe I'd seen it when the party started, or upstairs. A small, dim room flickered in my eye, and the baby falling, fallen. But that was a stupid idea, I'd never even been upstairs. The boys kept drinking, laughing. A couple of them I'd met before, but they didn't look at me. They'd only look at me if Bridget was around. A hand on my shoulder made me start. It was him. I stepped back with my hand up.

Don't *touch* me, I said.

Somebody left a baby, one of the boys said. But *don't* pick it up, it smells like shit.

Which made me glance down. Its skin grayish, with this funny hood pulled up, hanging into it blank, black eyes like a half ski-mask. It turned its head weakly like to shake the hood off but couldn't. It curled and uncurled its fingers and fists, groping at the dry dirt, its spine writhing weakly, its feet pawing at nothing.

Fine, he said. *You* deal with it.

He turned to leave but I didn't have to watch him, this wasn't my problem, the other Ruth passed out, the baby. It was somebody's problem, not mine. I didn't have to do anything; this had nothing to do with me. I didn't have to stay, there were guests everywhere. I wouldn't look at it again but I did. Its big deadish eyes gaping, the filthy blue suit it wore, its lumpy head rolling on a weak neck, its shit smell. It mewed, it didn't make a sound. I looked away quick and then all I thought was how simple it could be not to look anymore, to turn my eyes and body like this and walk or run away.

NINE

We were in the truck again, driving north toward town. We didn't talk. Bridget in the passenger's seat didn't try to hold her head up and I was still half out of my mind. I couldn't look at her, but I didn't hate her like sometimes. It was a beautiful morning. Maybe the smoke would let up. Just this once, maybe. Mist clung in the valleys and brushed the peaks. In some high places the light glowed softly yellow or pinkish, but the hollows, the narrow draws, the river bottoms, the little valleys still hung in shadow. Bridget directed her eyes unseeing out the passenger window at the Sapphires undulating on our right.

They were widening the highway. But it was Saturday and the machinery crouched like dormant monsters not breathing along the gravel shoulder.

Bridget pretended to sleep.

Otherwise we were alone. A Subaru passed. A Dodge Ram. And then in the shoulder some guy walking backward hitching. He didn't have his thumb out but he was asking for a ride. He looked familiar. Then I saw. It was the guy who'd gotten us out, off the dance floor. He wore an army-green canvas duffel and even at that speed he looked me in the eye. He raised his hand. I watched him in the rearview mirror, turning to watch the truck pass and then he threw both hands up like Fuck You.

Shit.

What? Bridget said with her eyes shut.

Somebody, I said. Some nobody from the party.

But he was already out of sight.

TEN

It was just past dawn and smoky. Empty highway, machinery, and me walking north in the ditch. Shit. My drunk turned hangover quicker than shit off a duck's back. A semi passed screaming, in my head screaming. If I took one step left I'd be dead, just like that. The semi's wake stirred the dust so I spun squinting and there was that Ruth driving a Chevy, Monroe in the passenger's with her head against the window looking rough. I reminded myself I'd left them by the side of the house because this was not my problem. There'd been guests everywhere, it was not my problem.

It's not like I was surprised—I'd been expecting them. But I hadn't decided what I'd do exactly, and here the moment was. My head ripping apart, revolting from my third eye out. All I wanted was a ride, I didn't give a shit who drove. So I raised up my hand like surrender or a command: Stop. Typical bitch move—they didn't stop, they drove right on by.

Eventually, this old guy picked me up. Carpenter, former hippie, smoking a Camel under his comb-over. I slid my pack in the bed, next to his chop saw. He was listening to AM talk radio but he put on Hank when we started to drive. He was driving to the job site, put in a few hours on a Saturday finishing up the trim at some Health Insurance Executive's dream house—nine-car garage, three floors, elevator.

He's building two this year, says the carpenter. Mansions that is. Shipped these five-hundred-year-old fireplaces in from France. But the place is ugly.

I didn't say anything. He laughed, coughed.

Free country, I guess, he says. Man makes himself a bundle on bankrupting a bunch of sorry sons-of-bitches who was going to die anyway, I can't say exactly that's a crime and anyway, guess I'd do better to keep my mouth shut. It's on account of him I'm working. I ain't gonna stop him.

Why bother, I said.

He grinned.

Not what I'd expect to hear outta some young punk, he said. Guess things ain't how they used to be.

He dropped me off by the hospital. I got my pack from the bed and went around to the driver's side where he had his window down.

Look kid, he says. In this valley things look like one thing. But underneath, everything's going in the opposite direction. He waved the cigarette at me, flicked it up the street, rubbed his forehead. You'd be doing yourself a favor to keep your eyes open, he says. Not all these hobos Midwest rich kids.

Took me off guard. If he'd said it mean I might've told him Fuck You. But he hadn't. And more than anything, I wanted to know what I had on to make him think I wasn't for real. He was looking in the rearview at the traffic. He put the truck in gear and I stepped back, up on the sidewalk.

Now you take care, he says.

His engine's combustion loud against the morning and his cigarette in the street. I looked around like I expected to see what he was talking about. But there was just the hospital like the Miniluv, the tallest building in sight with these black reflective windows, the kind that don't open. I started toward downtown feeling like hell, watching the cars. I guess I did know what he meant. The girls, the baby, the party. Seemed simple enough, but underneath there was something else happening, something that wasn't happening at all. Like they, *we* were inmates plotting the prison break in long looks, in backward glances at the warden. Only the cell bars were wildfires. Only what we'd done was nothing.

My pack was my cross to bear but at least the morning was cool. Be hot soon enough with the smoke thinning and the sun desertish. I looked up at it burning white in my eyes, knew I'd better set up camp before it got much hotter. Across the street some hobos crouching, slouching on this tidy concrete little wall, the courthouse behind them. They were just doing nothing, drinking. Didn't notice me across the street even though I was like them with my pack. Maybe that old hippie was right: I was different. I was making a statement, I wasn't just some nobody, some bum. What I did counted, heading out West, living under the radar, so no matter what somebody would notice, somebody was watching.

At the corner I stopped to think. If anybody knew where to pitch a tent, it was those sorry sons of bitches. Even from here, I could tell they'd been sleeping outside for years. And it'd made them mean-eyed, evil, and filthy with a black cloud above them, swilling from the bottle. But if what I needed was a place to sleep, it was them I'd have to ask. I started to cross without waiting for the light to turn. A low sedan braked, honked, and I put up my hand. The hobos saw me now. Licked their cracked lips, didn't blink or move. All their eyes watching, bleached by the sun. I made it across. I wasn't scared.

Hey college boy, one said.

He said it mean like he'd said retard. One in fatigues reading, one in a bandana, one big one, one long-haired. They were a mess of shopping carts and sleeping bags. Pick-ups passed. Tough-guys and pretty ranch girls stared. But the courthouse was on public land, nobody could tell them to get. Anyway the hobos didn't care who looked or who said what since the hobos had a bottle.

You got a cigarette, man, one said.

I stopped to look around at the false fronts and rooftops, then got out my tobacco pack and handed it down. Old white guy, long greasy hair. One eye wandered, I wasn't scared. I swallowed. I'd pictured hobos like traveler kids, punks, anarchists like I'd seen in Minneapolis. Tan, with combat boots and some kind of mohawk or dreads, looking good without a shirt. Or old wise-guy boxcar hobos reading Plato, or like a young Bob

Dylan. But these were filthy old criminals with bad teeth or no teeth and that death row look in their eyes. Two passed out in the grass so hard they could've been dead. Another one, a big one, tilted the bottle back to empty it.

You got a couple bucks, we trying to buy a bottle. And he laughed, big scar curled beneath his mouth like another smile.

I had cash in my wallet—a couple hundred. It was a nice wallet. Tawny calfskin. Newish with a tiny Polo stamped into one corner. I should've thought of that but hadn't. Shit. You could die, you could die, don't get caught. I wasn't about to get that piece of leatherwork out in front of this crowd.

Nah, I lied. Fuck if I had a couple bucks, I'd already *have* a bottle.

But Scarface knew. All those fuckers knew. With their eyes slit up at me, they just knew I lied. They could smell it. Almost as if they knew what kind of cash I really had, even with them so drunk. Their squint eyes watched me, their pale in the sun eyes like they'd killed a man. Scarface set the bottle on the cement and it fell.

Fuck you don't, asshole, he says.

I swallowed. I had a pistol. All wrapped up in a cloth and deep in my pack.

Nah? I said. I got some change.

Just trying to be honest, says Scarface. Ain't gonna lie and say I'll buy a sandwich 'cause I ain't. But I thought you'd be understanding. But guess you just another fucking little.

I could've walked. I could've forgotten the whole hobo scene, figured what you see is what you get and forgotten all about what that old hippie said like things would turn out different in the end. But I didn't. I would become what I wasn't. I'd morph right there in front of their eyes and they'd see what they wanted me to be. So I just stood looking this nasty bum in the eye like I wasn't afraid, like I had something to prove. Which I did. And that is that my pops had handed down a thing or two to me anyway. That I could do anything he would've done. Everything he'd done.

I *got* some change, I said like I didn't care for repeating myself. I reached down in my pocket, I had some quarters in my pocket.

All right. All right he got some change.

Dropped the quarters in the Scarface's hand.

Shit, he says. Shit, Reuben, this boy's rich.

Reuben was with the long greasy hair. His stray eye pointed at me. Without thinking I touched the Evil Eye tattooed behind my ear. Scarface counted the quarters.

What like five *bucks* in quarters. You wasn't gonna hold out on us, were you, college boy.

He grinned at me dirty. I'd done right and I gave a little smile.

Take a load off, college boy, he says. Take a load off. Get yourself a seat.

I looked around. My pops would've sat down. I dropped my pack. I've got nine thousand on my person, I thought. If only these hobo drunks knew it, unless they really do. I'd be dead so fast. We sat around on the little wall and this trashy blond guy with small eyes went to buy the bottle with my quarters and a couple bucks they had between them. I sat smoking one rollie after the other trying to look mean and watched the yuppies, the pretty girls walking or driving by keeping a lookout at us from the corner of their eyes. And I liked that.

I sat at the end of the line of them with my feet propped on my pack like I was taking a load off but I was guarding it. The old boys were happy to smoke my tobacco except one a couple men down with a little plastic baggie of half-smoked butts. He'd pick a good long one out of there and light it off the one he'd just finished. Then he'd keep reading the book he had open. I couldn't see the cover. He'd shaved his head, wore US army fatigues, and had a press pass written in Arabic. It must've been fake.

Smells like a campfire, I said for something to say.

That got the hobos going good so they were just a mess of hoots and coughs.

Campfire, college boy? Reuben says. That's *wildfire*. And it's coming for us. It's coming for *you*.

Made me start, the way he said it like he'd said Boo. And it made me mad.

I *know* it's wildfire, I said.

All right, says Rueben. You knew it. What, they teach you that in college?

He laughed. But the blond was back with the bottle and the old boys passed it all down the line so I was last. After Rueben. Which I pretended not to mind, it being my bottle and all. I took a good pull and hid the face I would've made.

You all know where a man can pitch a tent in this town?

Reuben gave me a look with one eye and coughed and laughed. Scarface coughed. The one with the bag of butts lit another. The boys passed out didn't move.

Used to be, Reuben says. Used to be you could've pitched a tent right *here*, right out front of the courthouse you had a mind to do it. But now. They got these ordinances and they got these new laws. Don't know what they mean to do to us.

So there's no place huh, I said. For camping.

But this skinny guy in a bandana—you could tell he was a vet just looking at him—with the palest blue eyes, he leaned forward.

I'm telling ya, brother, he said and blinked. And me with no place to *sleep*.

He staggered to stand and took a couple steps and stopped before me. False store fronts across the street framed his face. He held out his hand like to shake and I took it but looking him dead in the eye I was afraid. His eyes were everything and milky and hard, and looking at them the ground under me twisted away. All the old bums smoking my cigarettes and Richard,

Pops, everything melted toward me in his eyes. I glanced away. When I looked back he was still staring. Skinny fucker. Imitation Wranglers, beige military issue boots that looked like he didn't take off much.

I *served* in the United States Military.

He saluted and tried to click his heels.

Fourteen fucking years, he said. And look at me standing in front of you.

He grabbed at his neck with his free hand and pulled out his dog tags.

Desert Storm, he said. Desert Storm and I never fired without a direct order to do so. POW. Wounded on the field by those very I'd come to protect, yes.

I nodded and he saluted again. He still had my hand.

Shut the fuck up, Joseph, Reuben says. The kid don't want to hear your bullshit.

Reuben had the bottle and he lifted it slow and drank. I didn't think on the filth that hand was covered in.

I ain't no liar, Joseph said.

All right, I said.

I tried to take my hand back but it just made Joseph turn and look.

And what do I got now? Tell me, what do I got? I have lost every goddamn thing I ever had. I do not have no place to sleep. I do not have no bed.

I tried not to look.

I'm sorry to hear that, I said. I mean. I'm sorry.

Do you *understand* me, brother?

It was phrased like a question but it was a threat and meant I'd do well to look in his eyes and take everything from him. I could smoke soon, I thought, and felt a little better. I clenched my teeth and looked up at his two little open wounds for eyes, at nothing. At everything that rotted at the bottom of him and me.

White flecks grew fungal from a black center, swam in the pale blue ether. Blue ether white black nothing. That was all.

Yessir, I said and did not blink. I believe I do.

And I did. Because in his eyes I'd seen something most men never would. Which is what a million illusions this thing we named living is. You imagine you know what the sun is and give it a name that means nothing. Joseph grinned. Even if we all are, only the crazies, the lifers know how bad it is to be free, abandoned by God. But there I sat, falling. It was the only truth, and there weren't words for it. Reuben laughed, dropped the bottle, coughed long in his hand.

Hell you scared the shit out the kid, Joseph, Reuben said.

He wiped his hand on his pant leg and slapped me on the back. Joseph still had my hand. My body tingled. My palms, my ears, and armpits. I'd been infected. I knew I'd been infected. Like my soul was gone. So I was cursed, and I'd suffer like he'd suffered, some fuck-up scum nobody gave two shits about.

This boy. Joseph pointed at me. This boy understands. He *knows*.

He turned to me and didn't smile. Something in his look had changed such that it didn't scare me. Or maybe I was the one changed. Now I knew I was abandoned, falling, free, I didn't know what I would do, could do. It was a simple thing. I could reach out and touch what and where I'd been, but things had changed.

I took my hand back and rolled a cigarette, my fingers shaking.

The one with the press pass looked up.

You trying to camp? he said, as if I'd only just asked.

His voice was steady and he turned to look at me, his eyes warm and clear. He smiled and nodded once at me, put his book down.

Ben, he said.

He stood up part way and reached over the drunks with his hand out. Joseph staggered once toward him and started patting him on the shoulder. I took his hand and we shook. It was a simple thing. He was skinny and strong, like he knew how to work. Maybe he really was with some press on a crazy kind of assignment. *This* was what I'd had in mind when I'd pictured hobos. Men with a little mystery.

Some nice spots, Ben said. Close. Probably you're about done walking, that load.

He nodded at my pack.

Been a long way already. I said, Long night. About time I got some rest.

I hear you, Joseph said. Find some rest.

He sat down next to Ben, put his head in his hands.

Hellgate Canyon, Ben said. By the river.

He waved his hand to the left. I turned to look at two low mountains meeting. Shadow filled the gully that spread and twisted between them. The sun was getting hotter but it looked cool in there with swaths of blackish trees. Rough rocks, grasses. One low cloud rubbing the right-hand hill's flank.

Good folks stay back in Hellgate. Folks who like things kept simple. Understanding people. Everybody minds his own. Business.

I nodded all thoughtful and seriousness with my hands between my knees.

Just what I had in mind, I said. Just what I had in mind.

ELEVEN

Back in town I pulled up in front of my building but didn't turn the engine off.

I hoped we wouldn't make a big thing saying goodbye. The truck door took my arm swinging open and I jumped down from the driver's seat and stretched. Like always after a party I was feeling all guilty so I hung around and brushed at the dust on the toes of my boots. Soon she eased out of the cab and came over to where I stood. She hung to the inside door handle biting the inside of one cheek and looking at the ground. She was a little limp maybe, but gorgeous. I waited, glanced up at the simple horizon, the dried, brown hills, and inhaled dawn air, dew and exhaust and smoke invading. When I looked back at her she glanced up at me. Her eyes strained, her brow in sharp folds. She always cried after the parties. I didn't get it.

It was fun, she said.

I laughed a little with my arms folded. A tear down her cheek.

Yeah, I said but I didn't mean it.

Sorry, she said and wiped at the tear.

I shrugged. She could've meant anything and I tried to think of something to say in reply, something real maybe but there was nothing.

TWELVE

I walked the trail by the river past where two fly-fishermen stood thigh deep. The sun beat down and the day so dry even my sweat wouldn't stay. Passed the university football stadium on the right. Some kind of cheer practice going on but I couldn't see in. The PA played computer-generated pop music. Actual living people didn't make shit like that. It reverberated off the hill face. I was hot as hell walking straight into the dark, cool mouth of the canyon, those two little mountains growing on either side. The sunlight straight above grazing the mountain edge. The hill on the right had a big white letter M halfway up and some little dot-people zigzagging toward it.

At first I thought it was a storm coming from that side. A fat haze crawling up over the hillcrest swirling brown and yellow and reddish on its edges, the mass of it almost white. The wind picked up, and the haze billowed, engulfing the sky until it had swallowed the sun. The wind stayed high and I waited for the rain to hit. But it didn't come. The light started peeling from the edges, lengthened and narrowed like light in a cell. Then I realized. The storm cloud was smoke. My eyes burned but I kept staring at the sun, which shone dull and listless behind.

Soon I was beneath that little mountain, the earth heaving up as if the tectonics that made it weren't finished, and just beneath the surface of the visible the rock kept thrusting up. The river turned left and away. Wide river, clear. With a stretch of rapids right beside me, parallel to the mountain's foot, those rocks in the river probably fallen from it, avalanche. Couple kids floating downstream on inner-tubes with beers in their hands. Then they were up close approaching the rapids but still too small to make their faces out.

Two birds flew together over the river. Hawks maybe, but they could've been crows. The weeds grew tall on the banks, the sun disappeared. I was behind the lip of the mountain in shadow at last, but it didn't make my pack any lighter. The trail was wide and rocky. Then there was a cliff. Slimy water dribbled down it and a bum filling his bottle. His busted bike on a kickstand in the trail. He saw me coming and he stood up wild-eyed. He wore a trucker cap, filthy white sneakers, and a purple t-shirt under a women's anorak.

He was already behind me now. I hoped he wasn't following but didn't turn to see. In a minute I'd forgotten all about him. Goddamn it looked good out there. I didn't even mind the smoke, the eerie light. Because anyway three-quarter mile from downtown and here's this crystal-clear river and the mountains covered in dark pines and cliffs like you'd see on TV just jutting up all over the place.

Plus for Montana, this was nothing. A man was doing all right for himself camping in a spot like this, smoke and fire or not. So close to town with nobody hassling you—no assholes, police. Maybe I'd thought wrong about the girls, the hobos, me. Maybe this was a place a man *could* be free. And once I'd found a good spot I'd pitch my tent, drink a Blue Ribbon, have a good look at the river. There was a whole country out there. Hundreds and hundreds of miles all around. Mountains and wild people, wild land. Women. Monroe and her angry, sad little friend. I might see them again.

The smoke thickened and my eyes burned, my nostrils and throat too. My back all sweat under the pack and my hand swollen, throbbing in the heat but I could do anything and nobody would know shit about it, nobody could say a thing or stop me. I had the cash, I didn't need a thing from anybody, I didn't need anybody. I would make it because I was self-sufficient, I was free.

THIRTEEN

After dropping Bridget off I slept for twenty hours and in the morning I woke in a puddle of burnt orange light. What a difference a day makes, I hummed. Still there was something sinking in my stomach. But maybe things would be all right, things would be fine. My wallet next to the bed—I paused before I looked, to make sure. Two-fifty left, twenties, and some tens. I'd thought it was worse, but even that much wouldn't last long. I wouldn't look out the window at the hills on all sides, hemming me in, at the thick smoke that had returned ravenous to eat the sun. I would stay here and forget everything, starting now I'd begin again, I'd be new.

Someone was always watching. So I did what I could to remain composed. I stared at my clock and loved the nervous moves its hands made. I had no job, nowhere to be, so the time told me nothing. I'd found that clock in George's basement after I'd tried to kill myself but before he sold the house and I left for Montana. At the time I'd hoped he'd tell me it had been my mother's, but he just said he'd never seen it in his life.

George. My dad was probably smoking a cigarette and drinking coffee not reading the paper in his new condominium in an otherwise empty building watching the Mall of America and the weekend traffic studding the freeway, freeways and parking lots in every direction. If I killed myself, it was George I'd feel sorry for.

I got out a cigarette. Even with the windows shut I could smell the smoke inside. I was guilty, with a tightness in my chest. That was the thing about the parties, the guilt, lingering. It was the liquor, the pills and whatever. Made it hard to remember what you'd said or done. But it was good to smoke in bed. I rolled to my side and tried to think of what to write in the red spiral notebook. I could write about the party, try and remember what had happened. Or I could write some poems. Later. Later I would write. I would write nothing.

My phone was in the corner and it didn't ring. Usually Bridget called me at least once a day, but maybe now, now that she and Lydia and Audrey were so fucking close again she wouldn't. Not that I cared. Maybe this was my way out of this mess that was being friends with Bridget. I'd do fine without her, I'd be better off, I'd be free. I was a natural loner, I didn't need anybody. None of the good writers or musicians do. To them, other people are expendable.

I thought about how I looked. Maybe like an actress in an indie movie with books scattered on the floor, the red bedding. I could be a character in a movie like that. The way I dressed, the cigarettes, the pills, the parties, me and Bridget. Everything we did felt like a movie. But I didn't need her. I didn't look at the empty bottles in the corner. I didn't look at the trash can so full it overflowed onto the floor or at the stains on the floor and the bottles of beer, damp butts floating. Bridget's place never looked like that. Bridget's place was always so fucking perfect, photographable. All I had to do was clean this place up. Which I would if I could just fix this little glitch in me. Then I'd get up off the bed here and I'd be perfect. I'd be free.

I looked back at my books. My books were cool, movie-worthy. I had some Virginia Woolf by the bed. They'd belonged to my mother and were hard-backed. And Kafka, Plath, Anne Sexton. I believed in suicides. I'd spilled wine on some of the pages but I didn't think this was a cliché, if I really meant it. I could write like that, like any of them, if I tried. And I still looked good. Not like Lydia or Bridget, but I was skinny. I could drink and drink and not get fat, which was good. All I needed was a boyfriend. Then I'd keep my place nice, I'd get up and make breakfast for him or something. Then Bridget wouldn't matter. There'd been the boy at the party. But I knew what he really wanted.

In the bathroom I hung my head between my knees and pissed. My reflection was skinny and sick like I liked. I had some amphetamines in the medicine cabinet. Maybe if I took one, it'd fix the glitch and I'd be new then, afterward. One orange pill looked tiny and sexy on my fingertip. Maybe I'd clean my place up. It would look like Bridget's if I threw away the bottles. The pill so orange it burned, I took it with a palm of water.

My lips were puffy and red as ever. Bridget's mouth was more perfect than mine, which was too big, redder, horrible. That was like everything with Bridget, around her I was excessive, a mess. Even in bleach-blond she was flawless. Like Lydia and Audrey, perfect always. Totally fucking perfect. I didn't care if Bridget never spoke to me again. I didn't need her, I didn't need anybody.

In the living room I played Deltron 3030 who said, Secretly

plotting your demise. I was in my underwear. Maybe Bridget would call, wouldn't. Through the door in the dim kitchen dishes in the sink. But I didn't go in there. The living room with pictures stuck in neat rows everywhere on the walls, like black and white photos of the good-looking writers or rockandrollers I liked, a Schiele self-portrait with a grimace, *The Tower of Babel.* I could've opened the curtains but didn't.

I paced the room picking up bottles and arranging them on the dictionary. I admired the bookshelf from a distance, then up close. I said some titles aloud. *Capital of Pain*, I said, *Naked Lunch.* I pulled the pretty curtains open and squinted in the strange light. It was oily-gray outside, the smoke so thick I couldn't see the hills. It'd been clearer yesterday, but I'd wasted it asleep. I wanted to dance. So I picked the dictionary up without dropping the bottles and spun to the kitchen but at the threshold I stumbled and every bottle fell and smashed. My toenails were painted red.

I got a broom. The shards I left in the dustpan since I had to dance. But the song changed and it was *Indo Silver Club*, which is frantic and the kid in the cage had played it so I ran to skip it but a stray shard cut my sole. I fell back hard on my ass on the floor and squeezed the glistening piece stuck with blood into the soft flesh with the beat pulsing.

I turned the music off and got back in bed but I couldn't sleep. Even with my eyes shut party-guests' heads bred around me, their soft open mouths and wet eyes multiplying. Dusty red light from inside my eyes everywhere like the light in the house, red curtains over its windows. I opened my eyes so they would not multiply, so they would not watch me anymore, anymore, but it was sunset through the smoke so the light still bled and the guests would not stop. There was something in the grass by the side of the house. Bridget used her good mouth to smile. Everybody stared, hands clasped before their crotches.

But I wasn't doing anything, I said.

Bridget with her hand over her mouth.

You killed her, she said.

Everybody laughed. I stood alone and stood up fast and gasped. I was in the bath tub. The water breaking with me it swung in a single wave lapping my shins. Someone was watching. Someone was always watching. My head wet and the bathroom fading to a thin white light. I stepped from the tub before I could see again; I dropped wet footprints on the floor. In the bedroom I hobbled naked and endeavored to remember running the bath. Wrote a list. It was strange to write, the words unknown. Hummer. Lydia. Birthmark. Something by the house. I wanted a drink. A drink. The list made me remember. Unless what I thought I remembered I'd made up, which was possible.

In bed I was empty, I was nothing. I would disappear, the whole fucking world would just poof. Bridget hadn't called. Fucking phone like a tracking device, so Bridget could spy on me. Make sure everything was normal. I wanted a drink, I needed a drink but I couldn't get up. I lay and stared at the ceiling swirling, thought on nothing but my mind in spins, in fits and starts. I wondered what Bridget was doing, if she was alone. I flipped my phone and looked at its bite-size screen.

But I couldn't call Bridget. She'd be with Lydia and Audrey maybe. And she'd ask what the hell was I doing, and I'd say nothing. Or I'd say, I am just losing my fucking mind. So they'd say, She's desperate. Pathetic. Freak. And anyway that was not something I could say to Bridget ever. Even though it was all her fault.

If I called, if I tried to make her understand, I'd have to explain. Myself. And that I could not do. I'd have to explain about Lydia and Audrey, how they would steal her from me. Or about Bridget herself. The parties. That filthy baby. About the fires or this town. How we were trapped here, dead-eyed, docile. As if we'd get out after this. As if I'd get out. As if I'd make it out alive when there was nothing but this.

So I started to drink. I kept the liquor in the low cupboard, some Old Grand-Dad half full, some vodka. Then I was so angry, I was raging, a firestorm in me. My eyes burned. I seethed and sat in every part of that apartment. On the floor, on each chair, on the couch talking to myself and drank. I never remembered when I slept or which pills I ate but I scrawled in the red spiral but later I couldn't read any of it. I opened a curtain a crack and stared out at the smoky nights and days but there was nothing to see. The fire's haze across the streetlights, the bar lights, the headlights, the sun.

FOURTEEN

It was just some bourgeois trail out of town but those wild cliffs did still cover the hillside all sharp and rough-clumped in ragged towers like the top of a gothic chapel with the wildfire smoke like incense spreading skyward. I kept looking up all the time with the fat river down left. Then the bank spread wider with short trees across it and moved the river farther from me so its long lip was always hidden. The trail curved deeper into the shallow canyon at the place where the bum waited, where the dirty water dribbled from the rock. After a time a footpath disappeared down left into the brambles and I took it nearly slipping on the loose rocks in a tiny avalanche. The low gnarled trees scratched my face even while I held them off with my good hand.

In a clearing was some trash in a pile and a sleeping bag, three cut open water gallons propped against the burly roots of a tree filled with brown water. A fire pit with Sparks tall-boys and a couple bottles of Christian Brothers around it, which meant there'd been a camp here, but there was nobody around.

I could've used a cigarette but I went on, took the footpath as close to the river as I could, stuck to the shade. I sucked smoke with every breath and it was hot as hell. Yellow condos across the river, little shit boxes baking in the sun. Came to a low beach by the water and I scrambled down to it. Looked up and down the river and behind, sweating with my pack on. Kept on getting farther from the river again until I'd found a good little flat spot in what they call a glade or a glen and dropped my pack, my head pulsating with a dull pain.

I'd stuffed a six-pack of tallboy Blue Ribbons in at the top. I got one out and drank half. It was still cold and it made my head a little better. I took off my shirt and got my tobacco out for a rollie. My hand throbbed—the beer hadn't helped with that. After freight-jumping and hitchhiking, this would be the first time I'd sleep in my tent. I bought it used at Ax-man Surplus on the Midway in St. Paul, and after that I went next door to the Turf Club, a goodbye party for myself. I sat at the bar all night drinking bourbons with the tent in a green plastic bag under my stool. There was this noise show with a couple bands, some of that music you couldn't even listen to, just some kid with his shirt off screaming. But there was this Montana band, they sounded good. Fat girl singing, perfect drummer with a lazy eye, songs about chocolate cake. All night I'd talked to this regular with a gut drinking White Russians. I took it all as a good omen.

High weeds and brush grew around, hiding the trail and me from it. I started to spread the tent out, looking it over. Army green, a little beat up. I got it pitched and my pack and bag laid out neatly in it. Camp was set and it was only noon. I wasn't tired anymore, I had half a buzz started again and I was hungry, but all I had were the beers, I didn't have any food. So I cracked another tallboy and stood looking at the opposite edge of the river over the treetops. Nobody around but me and that river. River water. Silvery under the yellow condos, the highway and the railroad tracks on the other bank, behind a veil of smoke.

A footprint trail broke the bramble wall so I took my beer and followed it toward the water. At the edge the bank cut off so I had to scramble down to a scrap of beach maybe a foot wide, took off my boots and perched them on the hillside. I looked up river but there wasn't anybody. So I took off my jeans, hung them from a tree branch and waded in. The water cool, cold, heady until my feet ached. The bottom slimy and soft, and I dove. Water slipping around my skull, filling my cut hand stinging but good. I came up with a whoop, the current sucking me downstream. So I stood against it, the river-bottom slime in my feet's arches.

Yes hell yes.

Yes rose to a yell when I said it.

God, I said. Damn. God. Damn yes.

The current was strong, I leaned my shins into it. Fucking Montana. The cliffs cut the smoke that hid the sun. The hill left bore down on me. And this was only the start of it, one speck of the Rockies curling behind the smoke-screen in every direction. I watched the water froth and curl and rise around my knees, then swam hard into the current not going anywhere, little shrubs beside me. While I watched and swam in place branches brushed the water, leaves touched the water. The train screamed long, and then again. Sounding good like a forgotten memory, like The West was real.

FIFTEEN

Couple days later I was smoking a rollie, fishing with my good hand and this little pole I'd picked up at Fran's, a junk shop north of downtown, but I wasn't catching anything. It was stupid, me all wet from the thighs down like I thought this was *A River Runs*

Through It. I checked behind me, in case anybody was watching. But it's not like I was serious, mostly I just watched the water run. The river slid by, dragging the tip of my line downstream. But there were no fish.

Turns out my pops fished. I'd even found the pictures to prove it.

I hadn't been able to bring myself to look at those pictures after the first time, after I found them. But I had them in a ziplock, behind me on a boulder on the shore. It felt easier to look out here, in the open with the river slipping by like I could drop the stack right in if I didn't like what I saw. Or I could drop my thoughts right in, if it was them I didn't like.

I sat in the dirt and opened up the ziplock. This was the first one I'd seen, the wedding. My mom in a crimson dress with flowers in her hair and my pops with his shirt open and a vest, some little old hippie behind them wearing wire-rimmed sunglasses with purple lenses. My mom and pops both looking solemn, angry even, staring off at something to the left. Looked more like somebody'd died than their wedding day. But that old hippie in the shades, shit he was grinning at the camera like the Cheshire Cat, like he would up and disappear. Like he knew some secret, like he could see backstage, behind the curtain where everything was on display, where everything was in disarray.

Next, the one of my pops fishing, standing with the line in one hand, pole in the other, wearing Wranglers and no shirt, looking mean at the camera over his moustache. I could look like that easy. You could buy Wranglers anyplace, and nobody'd know the difference. Maybe it wasn't just the look I was after, but what he must've felt at that moment, a feeling, a man that was gone forever. It was like, religious, looking at that tiny copy of his face, and him almost dead in that picture. It was like looking at a saint, or a courtroom sketch. You could see it in his eyes, he was on fire. And he burned right up to the end.

I wondered who took that photo. It could've been my mom,

smiling at him from out of sight. But it could've been someone else. Could've been some friend of his, or another woman. I don't know what made me think of that.

There were other pictures too. Him and my mom, him with the tailgate of his rough truck open, holding a chainsaw, him and some skinny, mean-looking woman I didn't recognize, just standing there not touching. I didn't know a thing about him, his family—she could've been his sister, for all I knew. Next was one of him and that little hippie all Cheshire cat grin again, standing nipple-high looking up at my pops from below. Behind them was this cabin, looked like he'd built it himself, which was probably the case.

And then one I hadn't noticed yet. It was out of focus and all beat-up. My pops standing by a motorcycle, its engine in pieces on the ground before him. And my mom like she'd been smiling for the camera but had turned her head just as the shutter closed to look at that little hippie standing at the edge of the frame with a blue leather suitcase in his hand. Even with her face out of focus, I'd say her look was not one of happiness to see him. I flipped through the stack to see if the little man showed up again and he did, but mostly with his face half cut off, or with a hat that covered his eyes.

I could take a closer look but for that I needed a smoke. So I turned and made my way back to camp. There was a cluster of tall larch and I stopped on the skinny trail to tilt my head back and look up at the dark branches wandering in place. To look up at the edge of the glen where my tent was I stopped. There, sitting on a rock and sweating, wiping his shaved head again and again, looking all worn-out and staring hard at my tent with a little backpack at his feet was Ben, clear-eyed hobo with the fatigues and the press pass. Which was cool, it was fine. I hid the fishing pole in the brush with the photos. He didn't look up until I was right on him.

Hey, I said.

He had a good shadow going like he hadn't shaved since I saw him last.

Oh hey, he said. Man. Hey man.

Thanks for the tip, I said. This spot's great. Flat. Nobody around.

Yeah, he said. Yeah. I thought of you.

Didn't know what that was supposed to mean seeing as I was a stranger to him but I nodded. And he nodded, looking around at the clearing, which was narrow and longish, the size of a church. Bramble walls surrounded us and dappled the sun, giving the place a hidden, magical look. It was weird, how he'd just showed up. But I'd been solo for a couple weeks. I didn't mind a little company. Although if I'd picked a smaller clearing, just enough room for my tent only, maybe he wouldn't have found me.

It's Ben, right?

Had to move camp, he said. Had to. Smoke got so bad with that fresh fire down-valley. Not to mention that's horse country up there. Horse shit everywhere. So I get to thinking of this here spot.

Go figure, I said. Another fire?

Getting closer all the time, he said. Didn't know for sure you'd set up here. Smoke though. Doesn't agree with a person. Infiltrates the mind.

He tapped the side of his skull with his middle finger looking everyplace but at me. He got out his baggie of butts, lit one.

Yeah, I said. Tell me about it.

What's more, certain persons up where I was, talking. Started talking bad. Get to talking about *you* bad. Or me. Had to make my exit.

So what, it's a pretty rugged scene up there, I guess, I said.

He grinned in a friendly way and looked up at me for a flash. Smile lines around his eyes and his simple hands on his knees. Case of Pabst in the shade with my tobacco on top and I opened him one. Opened another, rolled a cigarette. I had my shirt off. Like my pops in the photograph. Ben seemed like a cool guy, a little jumpy. Sleeping around all those old hobos, psychos, it'd make anybody jumpy. He was older than me, a little over thirty. He looked at the beer like he was trying to remember what it was for. I laughed.

Thanks man, thanks. Hawk.

He'd said it like he really meant it and he took a couple sips pointing skyward with his free hand. I looked where he pointed and there was a bird, a hawk I guess, landing on a treetop a ways off.

Tastes good, he said. Didn't know of course you'd staked this spot. Didn't see the tent even, not till I got right down on it.

He was a bad liar.

Shit, I said anyway and drank. I don't own it.

Right on the river, Ben said. Rent free. Doing better than those *rich* assholes.

My hand tightened on the can to show me I knew he was not right. He stood and stretched to crucify himself but kept hold of the beer. I was just standing there not doing anything really, watching him all nervous like I was waiting for something big to happen.

Could use a plunge, he said.

He hardly looked me in the eye. Maybe that was it, the way he looked at everything but me that gave me this feeling like I was standing in an empty room waiting to see what was behind door number one. Maybe it was hell, or maybe my reflection.

Big sonofabitch that one.

He stared at the sky so hard that I followed his eye. Another bird circling at a distance. It shed oblongs of smoke and air while I pressed the open beer can to my lips but it was empty. I started toward the case for another. Ben ducked beneath the low branches that hung over the footpath toward the water. I watched him go with my hand in the case. The can was temperate and it geysered spittle over my knuckles when I popped it. I couldn't hear Ben in the brush anymore. I stood there drinking and scanning the treetops and the sky but I didn't see a thing with wings. I brought my drink and two fresh cans and the tobacco down to the water where Ben sat on his heels not moving. I set a beer on the rocky sand by him. He was fully dressed, didn't look much like he was ready for a swim.

You getting in?

Thinking about it, he said but didn't budge.

My arm's all right and I threw rocks in the current. Maybe he watched the rocks fall, but I thought he gazed higher, looking at something on the horizon.

You believe in your dreams? he said. In what you see?

I wasn't listening. I had Monroe in my mind's eye, her lips parted in an *Amarcord* snarl. Tossed her head once, the slut. Ben had paused to look inside my mind and watch what I imagined next, or to wait for my reply. Or else he was just talking to himself.

Ought to, ought not to, he said and nodded. Respectively. Only believe what you already believe. Like God is a perfect one and you ain't nothing but shit.

I only heard him after the fact but there was some truth in it, I knew first-hand even if I couldn't understand. My buzz had arrived, and what he said made me laugh.

Had that recently, I said all nonchalant. I mean I always knew my old man wasn't. I knew he wasn't my old man, I mean. An asshole like that he just couldn't be my dad. He's just a suit, you know. And come to find out, he wasn't. My dad.

I drank and crushed the can. Ben didn't blink, his eyes fixed on some fine feathered friend far-off. But I can't say I cared if he heard me or not.

Come to find out my real pops is dead anyway, I said. Died in a wildfire out here on his land I guess. That was before I was even born. And my mom had already left. Paris, I said and laughed. His name was Paris.

That made old Ben turn and look. Which I noted.

That's why I come here, and the way I said it sounded all right. To see what all I'd find out.

Name of Paris? Ben said. Wilbur's Paris. Dead man.

Yeah funny name, Paris. For an old back-to-the-land hippie cowboy.

Ben showed his teeth. It burned how he said it so hard and flat, Dead man.

Not read up on your Wild West history then, he said. It was one of the vigilantes by the name of Paris. Now there's people don't like vigilante justice. Call it terror. I can't say one way or another. But that's another story. Any case, plenty of rumors how that man Paris died. Some say it was somebody close to him did it, somebody he loved.

What, his wife? His mistress? I said and laughed, not really meaning it.

I hadn't really heard him until after.

Murder?

Maybe, Ben said. Some say it was political. Some say suicide. Like Wilbur, Wilbur says suicide.

Murder, I said and smoked.

Maybe I'd suspected something. Maybe it was why I'd come in the first place. He got his plastic baggie out and grinned at the butt he'd picked. Wilbur. I hadn't heard about any Wilbur from my mom, from Dick. That must've been the little hippie in the photographs, Cheshire cat smile. Like he was in on the joke. I was watching Ben's face as if maybe he'd know what I was thinking and tell me I was right. I hadn't noticed his teeth before: wolfish. Like mine? His eyes flicked up wild at me when I thought it, and back at the butt. The nails of his left hand filthy and long.

That's what we call hobo history, he said. Things you pick up along the way. But I don't necessarily keep the details straight. It's my mind's not strong.

He tapped at the side of his skull again with the middle finger. There was something he wouldn't say, something he didn't want to tell me. The stale cigarette smoke and wildfire smoke tickled his stubble and stank. We smoked. Across the water, a train, hazy in the smoke. The first cars were orange, the hill's sandy grass behind, the steel water, the whistle high and long and glossy. I didn't really see.

The son of Paris, he said. Paris. I suppose it's no surprise. This town's like that, hurries fate. Some call it a vortex. Like me, I'd say that.

I was nervous, I was laughing, pretending.

You gotta give me some context here man, I said. Vigilante justice I can get at the library. But it's my pops I'm here about. You said murder? I'd heard accident. But even so I came a thousand miles to see what there was to see. Anything. About his life. About how he died. How the fire got started. There's gotta be rumors about that. I mean, if there's something you know, anything, shit I'm all ears.

All I know. Is what I've been told. And that, he drank long from his beer and peered into it and smiled. Is a little. Hazy. It's other people who know. Wilbur. It's Wilbur who knows.

Something in the name.

Who is he anyway? Wilbur.

Little fellow, he said. Crazy fucker, but who isn't?

He knew my pops?

Best friends to hear Wilbur tell it.

I've got some old pictures, I said. Maybe it's Wilbur, I don't know. Little hippie. Kind of red hair. I'll show you. Let me show you.

He was already nodding when I went to get them from the edge of the clearing where I'd stashed them with my fishing pole, everything was gone. Pictures, pole, nothing.

Shit, I said. *Shit.*

I came back to where Ben sat stiff, staring out over the river at the train tracks that flanked it, at the highway, the condos.

My pictures, I said. The ones I was just about to show you. I had them five minutes ago. Somebody stole them. Just now. Somebody fucking *stole* them. You must've seen them. Right here, right behind me where I was sitting, you would've seen.

But Ben just stared like he couldn't understand me or like I wasn't there.

SIXTEEN

Soon it was Friday and the smoke still hung in the valley, so they encouraged residents to remain indoors. I was still in my apartment. Pacing, drinking less since when I did it made my throat close up. I was looking, watching the heads swarm the sidewalks. I was alone. I hadn't spoken for a week, not even on the phone, which made me think I was dead and didn't know it. I was nervous, guilty like I'd forgotten to do something important. Pay the rent, or the electric. I stood in the shower with my head down thinking, sucking water from the tips of my hair. A long time passed but that was nothing special.

I put on Levi cut-offs and an all but backless heather-gray Helmut Lang t-shirt, and my black cowboy boots without socks. I looked punk and skinny from not eating. I put on lipstick and a big canvas bag with my red spiral, my cigarettes, and my phone, watching myself in the mirror. I looked all right, I looked fine. Which seemed backward, not right, like I should look how I felt—like shit. I went into the kitchen and ran some water over the crusty plates and bowls in the sink. Poured myself a finger of Old Grand-Dad in a lowball and drank that. I took out a cigarette and matches but didn't light it.

I stood looking at the back of the front door, which I'd painted like kryptonite. I had a little mirror hung on it at eye-level and I checked my eyeliner before I put on my sunglasses and put my hand on the doorknob. Turned it. The door opened. Homeless guys are always passed out on the stairway and it stank like piss. I didn't inhale until I stood on the sidewalk, and then I was breathing concrete. Through the smoke the hobos across the street looked impressionistic. A cruiser passed, the cop inside turned to stare. Flecks of white ash gathered on one shoulder. The matchbook hot and damp in my hand and I opened it, lit the cigarette, and shook the flame out.

Even through the murk the mountains rose darkly in thick stands of evergreens over the tops of buildings. South was the Bitterroot Valley that stayed warm with sun all summer. But now it was burning, as close as Victor. There weren't any new fires north, which was the mountain, and the Rattlesnake Wilderness that followed the creek and spread hundreds of miles through Glacier into Canada. I could turn right and start walking, walk right out of the smoke, out of everything. I could walk for months and not see a single fucking person probably, keep walking until winter came and I starved or froze, curled against some sheer cliff somewhere, nowhere in the Rockies. Without a job nobody would even know I was gone. Nobody but Bridget. That still happened, people lost in the wild, frozen, drowned, dead.

Hellgate Canyon at my back. They said a pack of wild horses lived there, but that was just a lie. From a distance Hellgate looked vacant, but up close it was obvious how many bums camped there. Not horses. Not wild. Hellgate was tent city in the summer, it was no refuge, no escape. It had nothing to do with the wild the way the Rattlesnake did. The bums, or maybe it was the canyon, infected the valley, made it sour. Even the yuppies couldn't ignore the bums all the time, mean-eyed and passed out downtown, too drunk to make it back to camp. It was such a small town. So there were too many drunks yelling at the cars, or asleep or dead on the curb to always pretend things would turn out all right.

I tried to eat a slippery fish taco at the counter facing the window and watched the drunks smoking cigarettes around the door of the Oxford where they've got a twenty-four-hour poker game, fried cow brains served anytime, and the only hookers I'd seen in Montana. Back outside the smoke was an assault and I started walking, as if there was somewhere else to go. But I'd forgotten where I was headed, if I ever knew. So I changed directions, and then again, and once more and I was walking back the way I'd come. So it seemed funny I hadn't already noticed, just past the Oxford, a woman sitting on the curb with her feet in the street.

I don't know how long she'd been singing. I walked closer but didn't cross. With buskers it was better to keep your distance. A truck passed, and another. But her voice carried, filled and dashed, and immediately she fell on her knees, right there on the tar of the road. Her beautiful pale face was dirty with a dark dull mouth and one black tooth. She wore a crimson scarf and she was almost weeping, but so it came out melodious. Her very slender wrists. She sat back on her heels and sang.

Even though the smoke made constant twilight, the day was hot and she'd dressed for cooler weather. Watchers behind a thin screen of smoke, or she was, everybody's eyes devil-red. Mine were watering and rough like I was crying but I didn't. A soft cotton pale skirt gathered antiquely around her bent legs. A burnt yellow blouse belled at the sleeves and gathered at the wrists again. Three small buttons pointed to her strange face. She wore another shirt beneath—pale lilac cotton—and it clung to her throat. She rose slightly, her figure fluttered.

Behind her, hitched to a broken mountain bike was a

handmade aluminum trailer piled high with suitcases and brightly colored blankets and homemade furniture. Tacked to it was a hand-painted sign that read: Hands off. Big Brother is watching you. Just behind the woman stood a little man with a fiddle dressed in an out-sized corduroy blazer and an orange toupee. His eyes were conspicuous, crystalline, and nearby sat a perfect blond baby with its fat fingers on the blue velvet edge of a fiddle case, a single dollar bill inside. Its cheeks were pink milk and it stared straight at me before it turned its face up, but there was only smoke above.

It was lunchtime and the sidewalks swarmed with people so a crowd had gathered on the opposite corner. But they hadn't come to watch, they were waiting for the light to change. The baby scrutinized them, but the tiny man only saw the woman. When she sang he played, and when she stopped he was silent.

People started to cross, watching from the sides of their eyes but nobody stopped to listen or drop change in the case. The crowd was typical: a dwarf woman shuffling, her face hidden inside her hood; two blood-red boozers in longish hair and lazy eyes; an old tranny I knew from the library; a couple of dried-up party girls in thin shoes. Only one cleanish, rich-looking traveler kid stopped a few feet away to listen but I couldn't see his face. I could tell he was a traveler kid by the militaristic outfit, by the well-placed dirt on his hands and his pants, by the tattoo behind his ear I could see even from here. The Evil Eye. He didn't watch the woman, he only had eyes for the old man.

I could've crossed the street and gone up behind him and touched his shoulder and pretended to be bold, like Bridget. I could've been surly and coy like I'd already been. I could've apologized for not giving him a ride and explained. Or I could've said I didn't remember half of that fucking night and laughed. And then I'd offer and buy him a drink at Charlie's. And maybe it would've been all right, good even. I hadn't thought much of him, but now. I had to look at his face, I had to talk to him, but I couldn't, I didn't. I didn't do any of it. Then he turned.

He looked in my eyes, his were devil-red too, blackish and hard, he didn't smile. It wasn't just the party. It was as if... He raised his chin like, Hello beautiful. And paused. But then he turned back, and started toward the old man with his hand out, ready to shake.

But the old man wouldn't stop shaking his head like it couldn't be true. He let the fiddle drop and stepped back, and again, like what he saw before him was dead. The expression on that old man's face. Like it was something private, something I shouldn't be watching. So I looked down and in my hand I held a dollar. I couldn't remember getting it out. I ought to give it to the woman, I thought, but that would mean crossing the street twice, and waiting for the light to change right next to them and whatever domestic disturbance they had going. So instead, again, like always I turned and walked away like I wasn't watching, like there was nothing to see, like nothing could change from this moment for forever.

SEVENTEEN

It might've been days since I'd eaten. But I didn't set out for food, I set out because there was something I would discover. So there I was, walking by the river, weaving through the bushes throwing trash in the water. Beer bottles, gas station burger wrappers, a truck tire that took both hands to dislodge from the underbrush. Then back up to the fat path, the sun falling, casting the smoky sky in white-gold at the edges and a violent violet gray-blue in spots.

I must've been drunk.

I'd reached the stadium and there was a high wind, the clouds all white and weak above me. They strained from the edges of the sky, desiring each other, to catch the wind, and to gather to make rain. I sweated and watched, willed them to touch and turn dark together and let water down. For a long time I stood with my head and neck cocked looking up until I rolled a cigarette. I smoked thinking, Let a little rain down. God. Damn. Let in a little rain. I hadn't known I wanted it so bad until that moment, but it didn't make any difference what I prayed to God for or not, the sky kept silver as a prison cell one-way mirror.

The wildfire wind brought the smoke again and I was walking. Going slow in a drunk's swagger and scoping the guns in the pawn shop windows. It took some time getting from one side of downtown to the other. When I'd made it to the bars and the taco joint, the first thing I saw wasn't the man but the cart. Parked by the Oxford, hitched to a mountain bike. It wasn't the cart itself that caught my eye, it was the furniture and bright blankets stacked on it. Blood-red and hot-green and orange. And handmade wooden chairs, a chest of drawers, a table. A tiny household, packed tight enough for a bike to tow. The man was tiny like an elf, and he played the fiddle looking around him all the time. Something in the shape of the eyes, their color too blue. Like he'd walked out of my pop's photographs, all Cheshire cat grin. It made me start, to see a ghost. He stood nipple-high and rocked with a strain in the music he played, his woman on her knees singing. There was a child too, more than a baby, and fat with bright eyes like the sky as I remembered it.

The sound was deep for a fiddle and met the woman's voice at a wail. It rushed and slowed and slammed one part against the other like the freights crossing the plains and the mountains. Trains being a rare sight these days but one I'd seen, so I knew this song owned it. Even though I couldn't understand the words I knew in my drunk heart it was a mourning song, a song for love of the world although it was lost.

I hardly noticed I was walking closer. I looked around to get my bearings, and there, across the street, stood the girl from the party, forlorn little Ruth limp in the dismal light. It was a small town thing, or like a movie to see her again at this moment. Still it made me start. Like maybe it was a sign: him, her. I missed twelve beats readjusting the story to fit the fiddle and her, standing there. And turned back, started walking again. I watched the little man play without seeing really, remembering something in my mind's eye that I couldn't quite be sure of, someone else's memory. Eventually, he glanced up at me over the fiddle so I raised my hand like hello or thank you. He stopped before the music did, glaring, staring so I touched my chest.

It was the drunk delay, so now I thought, He knows me.

Wilbur? I said.

I didn't think before I said it, before I started, I didn't plan ahead. I don't know why I said it, I'd only heard the name Wilbur for the first time that afternoon. I'd only just heard Ben say, Suicide, murder. And here I stood, looking right at a photograph come alive. It had to be him, Wilbur. Just like that, no waiting, here to answer all your questions, the only man who can. Like Hollywood would. His eyes puckered shut, and he smiled. Cheshire smile.

Wilbur, I said again.

I had one hand up still, like I was saying stop. He took a step back and then another, and shook his head no. No. No. No. But he didn't deny it, it had to be him.

I knew you'd be back, he said eventually.

You know me? I said. You're. Wilbur?

He smiled grimly, but he wasn't really looking.

I. I need you to tell me what happened.

But he just shook his head, shook his head stepping forward and back and forward and back. I couldn't fucking understand it, like retards—the redundancy, the wagging, the back and forth that makes it too clear what every one of us does always, always.

Back and forth, spawning, scrawling, screaming, stalling. Here we go around again again again again. But at least a person could pretend. And he would not.

All night till I can't sleep, he said.

Which meant nothing to me. But I didn't ask because he kept on, swayed side to side, slicking his lips with his pointy, soggy tongue.

All these years I can't sleep ever again. And now you're here in daylight. And now you're here to take my days. To taunt me.

His voice at the end broke, desperate. The baby looked up at him. Funny how fear was so obvious on a thing that couldn't talk. Whereas I only blinked. I wasn't afraid. It had to be my drunk that kept me from asking him what I'd missed.

Now you're here in daylight, he repeated. You want we should do it all again?

It was a threat. His less-than-nothing eye upon me, swallowed me whole like I was already dead. Now I *was* afraid. Afraid from way back in, the place only Joseph had seen. I was up close to the man now, not a foot from him. His breath rasped, his weak chest heaved, he snatched his collar, his lapels, his fiddle-free hand convulsed across his chest. It was more than I'd bargained for.

I hadn't noticed his woman wasn't singing anymore. I didn't notice until she had one hand on me, and pushed me back from him. Now I saw her: weak, desperate, and poor. She had the baby in her arm. Now it saw me: drunk, alone, and burning.

Get *off*, she said. He's dying, can't you see? He's had a stroke, he's not well. He can't defend himself, it's not right to frighten him. Can't you see? He doesn't want to talk to you. He has nothing to say to you.

But I know him, and he knows me. Ask him. *Ask* him.

Her free hand gentle on his shoulder, but she was looking at me.

Knows you? He says that to everybody. He can't tell the

difference anymore. Every person passing on the street reminds him of somebody, something, anytime or place besides this one, now. It's *dementia*. He doesn't know you, it's just a dream.

She flicked at the air.

But he was friends with my dad, my dad Paris.

Which made her stop, her faced dropped. So I kept on.

I mean, I just learned about it today, about Wilbur. I didn't know my father. I came a thousand miles. And I just thought he could tell me. Who my dad was. Or. Or. Anything.

But she'd pushed me back again, harder this time. It caught me off guard, which was just the booze. The baby with its arm around her neck. Pointed its tiny finger, but not at me. Just behind her Wilbur stood staring through me whispering, his eyes that blue.

Get out of here, she said. Why you want to worry an old man? Leave us alone before I call the cops. There's one parked just there, been watching you this whole time. Like they're after you. How do I know you're not dangerous? I don't know you, I've never seen you in my life.

It was true, there was a cruiser idling, the cop staring straight at me.

But my father, I said. I just want to find out. Who he was. Anything.

If you really want to know, go ask his *other* woman. Or their child. You want to know what kind of man he was? You ask them, and leave a dying man *be*.

EIGHTEEN

I walked to Bridget's without calling. She was bleary-eyed, sitting on the steps of her apartment sipping a sugar-free Red Bull.

Her eyelids half up, she raised her chin a bit like Hello when I arrived at the end of the walkway, even though she'd been able to see me for a block already and was watching the whole way. She looked pale and wore a sailor-striped bikini top and store-bought cutoffs. There was a towel in the yard, covered in grass clippings.

Tanning? I said.

I pointed at the towel like, Trashy. She smiled weakly and I felt sorry for starting off mean.

Just a joke, I said and sighed.

I sat down next to her and smiled back. She reached out as if to hug me but then she touched my shorts lightly and flicked my boots instead.

God. *What* is happening with your outfit? Then she said, There is *no* sun.

I took out a cigarette.

I was trying to tan before work, she said. Like last *week* before they came to cut the grass. But even then when the smoke was lighter it was too thick to tan really but I left the towel out just in case I decided to try again tomorrow, last week. But I didn't. I forgot all about it. About the towel.

Bridget usually stayed on top of things, like a towel in the yard.

Would you grab it for me?

I looked from the towel to her.

You want me to pick up your towel for you?

Oh come *on*, Ruth, it's not that hard.

It looked like she'd been crying, although she was still gorgeous like always, so I got up and walked over and picked up the towel. It was white and navy striped, matching her bathing suit, and it said Ralph Lauren in a light brown that was supposed to look like gold. I shook off the dried grass clippings.

If it wasn't that hard, I said, why didn't you pick it up yourself?

It was just to get her to say *something*. Something mean, something normal.

That girl Ruth's dead, you know, she said.

She drank the Red Bull like she was smoking a cigarette, in little bursts to intimidate me. Her toes slowly curled and uncurled around the step. I tossed the towel next to her and she half-flinched like I'd thrown something at her that might hurt. Her toenails were painted pearly-white.

What? I said.

That girl Ruth is *dead*, she said. She like, asphyxiated. Isn't it awful?

My inside fell.

Didn't anybody do anything? I said. Didn't anybody help her?

Obviously not, Ruth. Obviously.

I'd seen her. I'd been right beside her. But I walked away. I left her to die.

Nobody helped her, Bridget said. I mean, what were they supposed to do?

Anything, I thought. I could've done something. Bridget stood up, turned to go back inside. But this was more than I could take. I stood too and I would've looked at the sky or the horizon, something that would remind me the world was tall and we all were small, but I couldn't see the mountains, or the buildings even, all I saw was smoke. Which meant I saw nothing but inside this shitty mind that made me turn and walk away from some chick and a fucking *baby* about to die. Not the baby. The baby wasn't dead.

It had to be a joke, it was a joke, Ruth. From God or Bridget, I didn't know. I didn't know what I was supposed to have done. There were other guests. Her friends, and the boys drinking. Maybe one of them was her boyfriend. But I doubted it.

Her place is a little house with refinished floors and original woodwork. It was always immaculate, all her pretty things. It was dark inside, the curtains drawn against the smoke. They were curtains for girls like Bridget: unmarried, Vogue beside the toilet, facials, uppers in the morning, tranquilizers before bed. When my eyes adjusted I looked through the doorframe into the living room. I was shocked or grateful because the room was torn apart. The papasan chair capsized and its cushion on the floor, torn into. The couch at an angle, the cushions on the floor, their plasticine fluff erupting. This is it, I thought. Maybe it was the police. Maybe they would come and interrogate me too. And I'd say, Yes, I saw her with her head lolled back and no shirt. Yes, I walked away. This means it's the end of it all, I thought. Either I'm done for. Or I'm free.

I was thinking too hard about what I saw, too deeply for what was before me, and what I'd just been told. Maybe it was shock? There was Bridget's framed Richard Avedon photo of Marilyn Monroe morose and innocent in a dark dress. There was something about that picture that had always struck me as fake. Like it was Bridget's attempt to prove she was the same kind of real-glamour girl as Lydia and Audrey. But she wasn't. She was just a townie with a dead dad and trailer park mother. And now that picture was on the floor, the glass smashed and the frame cracked. That was what Bridget wanted: to be the reproduction of that syrupy, mousy face, but shattered. It was pathetic, really.

Holy shit, Bridget. I was trying to drum up emotion.

Was it the police? I said, like I'd been drugged. Did the police come?

She came into the living room behind me with a fresh Red Bull.

The police?

Her voice clear, like nothing could touch her. She laughed.

About Ruth, I said and shook my head. The other Ruth.

The police don't know what to do, she said. But they don't have any reason to talk to *me*. I didn't have anything to do with it. I wasn't there. It was her own fault anyway. If she couldn't handle it, she shouldn't have been at the party in the first place. And now, she's dead. She's ruined everything. They've like, blocked off the house. The police are trying to *stop* the parties. That's like, against the constitution.

She pushed the cushion-less couch back against the wall and sat down, tossed one slender leg over the other one; a perfect, unblemished girl on a shredded, trendy sofa.

Isn't it? she said. What is that? The first amendment?

You've got to, I said. Fight. For your right. To party?

Our smile was sly; we were the real deal. We'd been in it together so far, driving through the endless land in her vehicle. I remembered all the best scenes now, and she did, I could see recollection in her eyes. The pills we'd split or shared, the cigarettes, the slew of fools swarming around us, us gasping for breath and drenched in sweat laughing, us laughing in our faces at how we'd been sabotaged. We were in this for life.

Anyway, she said. I was trying to call Lydia to see if she'd heard, and I just could *not* find my phone, she said. I was looking everywhere. I was totally. Trapped.

Your phone, I said.

She laughed a little. I guess that all the me-and-her-times didn't make a difference now. We were back where we'd started, with the Red Bull and the dead Ruth. Which meant I was free to look down on her. Which meant I was dangerously free, from God et cetera. And I thought, It's sad, how she'd make such a lame excuse.

You don't have to say that you know, I said.

With disdain. I sat beside her, partially turning my body away.

Yeah, she said not listening. And you know where it was?

I looked at the cushions, at the hidden white-white center those jagged holes exposed. Why hadn't she ever called me to say: Ruth is dead? Ruth was me.

Lydia? I said.

In the bathroom, she said.

What?

My *phone*, Ruth. That's what I was saying. My *phone* was in the bathroom.

Okay. Okay.

She could be vacant if she so desired. I was just telling her things were all right, that it wasn't our fault, we'd been at the parties all the time and never before had we seen a thing like this go down. I was *telling* her, or she'd been telling me. I was telling myself.

Guess I'll have to pick up around here sometime, she said.

It was unlike her, to neglect the beautiful, the material. She sighed but didn't move.

Her little living room. Low ceilings and cabernet walls. They'd been chic when she first painted them, but with the curtains drawn the lighted slats of dust made the room a cell. The other Ruth was dead. I wasn't surprised. And here was Bridget beside me, her hair blow-dried and her toenails painted. But I knew she was a mess. She bent to pick a couch cushion from the floor. She suffered, but what could I do? She'd hurt me so many times already. Now that all was gone.

I tried sounding noncommittal.

So you, I said. You called Lydia?

Don't be like *that*, she said.

I just didn't know since when you guys were friends again is all, I said. I didn't know you'd like, go to her, if somebody, somebody *died*.

Not that I cared. It was better for me anyway, for Bridget to sob, cling on somebody else.

Whatever, she said. If you're mad because I didn't call you. You didn't even know her like we did, since high school. Her mom was like, a social worker or something. I'd have to go talk to her, once a month. So I mean. Don't *be* like that. We were *close*. It's not like you're from here.

I'm not being like anything.

I just can't be like holding your *hand* all the time is all, she said. You can be really needy, Ruth.

It's just. It would've been nice to *know* is all.

But I just *told* you.

She sat staring just past me holding the Red Bull, her eyes blank.

No more parties, she said. No more parties.

I looked where she was, but saw nothing. Like I wasn't there, or she wasn't.

NINETEEN

Only a couple days and we had a regular hobo camp going. I'd attracted them like moths to a flame. The smoke cleared slightly in the night so a body could almost breathe. I was in my tent trying to think. I had to find the little man again. And I'd make him tell me what he knew. What he'd been talking about. If I still had the photos, I might find clues or something. Then I'd know what I was looking for. But I didn't have the photos because somebody fucking stole them. You'd have to be a real asshole to steal something like that, something that meant nothing to anybody but me.

I pulled from the bottle, fresh fifth of whiskey.

Like they were trying to stop me. But it wouldn't work. Nothing was going to fucking stop me. I'd have to find another way. So I started to read the letters I'd found, letters my pops had sent my mom the first time she left him. He wrote her nearly every day then, mostly about the wood he'd milled. To prove he was working like a dog and not doing anything he ought not. Or anybody. He just talked about what he and Wilbur'd been up to, like Wilbur was his chaperone.

Or my pops would get to describing some stick of wood like crazy, like he was in love with it. He hadn't been much for writing, hadn't left much behind for documentation as far as I found. But wood he could go on about forever. That and apologies. Seemed like he was always saying he was sorry, but never for what. He'd just say it would never happen again. I'd always figured he'd meant drinking, I hadn't thought of another woman.

I fell asleep with the letters in my hand. The predictable thing would've been to dream some big epiphany about my pops. Like his ghost at the foot of my sleeping bag all, Son, if I could've done things differently. But it never works out like that in real life, and instead I was dreaming about a girl, about Monroe like I knew I would. She was laughing at me, all gorgeous flicking that bleached hair at the top of a hill above me. Even in my dream there was smoke, the light came through it at a slant, and I looked up at her from below.

Must've been the laughing from outside my tent that made Monroe in my dream laugh, that woke me. Funny how you'll dream about somebody. I didn't talk much with the traveler kids in camp. They were real dumpster rats, picking lice, mean as the old-timers, prison tattoos on their faces. They weren't like me—they'd been born trash. For them it was either trailer park or this. One of them was Bong and he had one nasty dreadlock but otherwise his head was shaved. His girl they called Larch or Lurch and she didn't have any hair at all. I didn't know the other ones.

I flipped through the letters like something might jump out at me but nothing did. Looked up at the flimsy green roof of my tent. If I could get the photos back. Or I could go to every mill my pops had worked and ask around about him. Every place he'd lived, the burn site where he'd died. Where he'd been killed. Maybe. My mom hadn't said anything about a murder. But then, I hadn't asked.

I pulled from the bottle.

Or maybe there'd be something in the paper from back then. That made me laugh. Shit I was like, a fucking private investigator. Private dick. I pulled from the bottle.

I got my cash out of the little hidden pouch I'd sewed into my pack and started counting to help me think. Or maybe I just liked sitting with piles of hundreds and fifties in front of me in the green light reflected from the tent walls and the bluish light of my little lantern. It felt good counting like I was going to figure something out, like I would get to the bottom of it all. The cash was reassuring, since if I got in a pinch, it wouldn't be for long. I'd buy my way out. Plane ticket, bus ticket, bribe. Bribe.

Which made me think of Richard. Us in his office, him on his squashy, womanly ass, me with my fist on his big wooden desk. And he said, You ready for the truth, son? Like he was a tough guy, knew everything. Like I was his. And then he laid it all out for me. I don't know how he thought I'd react but for how fast security showed up he must've hit the panic button before I'd landed the first punch. I smiled and pulled from the bottle. Brown liquor in a wave against the side of glass.

Dumpster rats out there laughing, laughing maybe at me in the night like they weren't scared of anything, like they were real and I was just a fake. Bong. Lurch. The other ones. But they didn't know what I'd done, would do. Like steal for real, like kill a man. I pulled from the fifth again and got the stacks of bills together. They could do or say what they wanted, and laugh. I was in some real shit here, I was in a fucked up situation. Like from a movie, or a book and what were they?

The whiskey bottle upright against my pack. Then from the side of my eye I saw a vermin scurry across the edge of my tent. I stood up quick. Which spilled the bottle, me all hunched up under the low tent roof muttering.

I thrashed around, looking for that little rat I'd been trapped with unknowing. But there was just a mess of bills, thousands in bills all in disarray on the bag. And the whiskey spill, a liquor lake with its strong sour stink. I folded the bag in half with the cash inside and tossed it to one side, moved my pack, looked inside, swallowed, and stuck my hand in to feel for it, but there was nothing there. I held real still, I was breathing hard, held my breath. Nothing.

I unzipped the flap and beat my way out, stood up in the dark sucking at the smoke until I choked. The blue light dim and all wrong shining from inside the tent through the open flap since the lantern fell. I got my tobacco out to roll a smoke. And there was Bong and Lurch, the other ones behind and Ben with his hands between his knees.

Shit we thought you was having a seizure in there.

That was Bong. I lit the cigarette.

Nah, I said. Nah thought I saw a mouse.

As soon as I said it I wished I hadn't.

On cue they all laughed, all except Ben who hadn't moved.

A mouse? said Bong.

He passed the bottle and Ben took it and drank.

Guy says he thought he saw a mouse, said Bong. We thought you were having a seizure in there.

You said that.

Excuse me? Bong said.

What's that you got in there? Ben said.

But I only half heard him, I was watching Bong. Who was one of those angry, confused assholes who'd done too much PCP, drank too much whiskey. Trailer trash by birth and beat up by his dad and granddad and uncle and big brother so he'd gone crusty punk. So he'd gone dumpster rat and jumped on every word that came out of anybody's mouth like it was an insult. I will tell you I was scared of Bong, and he knew it. He could smell it, and Lurch, and the other ones, three other ones in the dark who were built like me with tattoos all up their fingers and arms and necks and squint eyes laughing hoarse and lewd. Ben stood up, took a step in the direction of my tent.

I glanced back over my shoulder. I'd left the tent flap open, you could see right inside where the money was all strewn about. I didn't wait to discern what was seen exactly. I took the two steps to zip it shut fast. Ben still stood behind me. I turned and walked toward him to keep him back. I patted his shoulder roughly but he wasn't looking me in the eye, he was still staring dead ahead like my body and the tent were nothing and whatever he'd seen was still visible. He must've seen the money.

Don't want to let the bugs in, I said. Good eye, Ben, thanks for the heads up to shut the flap, I mean ya'll distracted me half drunk you know but I wouldn't want to wake up with West Nile. Insects, larger biomass than the human race, et cetera.

Don't want to start a fire, Ben said.

Without knowing it I'd rolled and lit a smoke.

Your lantern fell, Ben said. You'd better upright it before your tent catches fire. Before Hellgate starts on fire. Make yourself a whole mess of enemies that way. People just about can't handle another fire. Transformation underway already. You start another one, there's no telling.

He had his hand up, just in front of his chest. He gestured making jerky, rough flourishes with his fingers and his palm. But I wasn't listening, all I cared was if he'd seen the money, as if I'd be able to tell by looking. It was the smoke that made his eyes hard to decipher. Always the smoke. The dumpster rats were whispering. He smiled once, very quickly before it faded. He'd shaved a few days back, all that was left was the shadow. He shook his head. Paw of Bong heavy on my shoulder. And he pulled me back roughly like I was trying to fight.

Hey guy, step off, right? he said and turned to Ben. You need rid of him?

I hadn't noticed I was panting fire with my hands in fists, standing this close to Ben like I would choke him. But Ben shook his head, no, and laid one small hand on Bong's fat-heavy chest. So we were touching, Bong, Ben, and me like New Agers on a spiritual retreat, not drunk hobos on the verge of a fight. I stepped back.

All right, boys, I said and faked a yawn. I'm beat as shit. I'm turning in.

And unzipped and rezipped the tent flap so there'd be no more seeing in.

TWENTY

I couldn't keep track of the days. They were hot and dry enough to call it drought, and then the wind started. Forty-mile-an-hour winds whipped up the canyons all down the Bitterroot Valley, pounded the fires past Victor, up Mill Creek, and west of Hamilton. Blew them up like crazy. Two hundred thousand acres, three hundred thousand acres charred. The firefighters didn't stand a chance. I stayed inside mostly. Like the old-timers, all day at Butterfly Herbs Café, all night at Charlie's, trying to conserve funds drinking rail liquor and coffee. I had about one-fifty left.

So it must've been afternoon. Because I was drinking coffee in the mini booth at the end with my back to the window. I was trying to read some Virginia Woolf. But I'd been drinking Seven and Sevens the night before which at Charlie's means stiff, and my head wouldn't work right. In my chest, in my throat all I could feel was liquor-fire, in my mind all I could see was the other Ruth with her head lolled back. I was wearing vintage YSL and crimson sharp-toed flats. The dress was a Safari style; it didn't fit well.

The skinny kid who worked the Butterfly counter during the week had made a sculpture of an angel with bedsheet wings, and he'd propped it in the window just behind my table so it partly blocked the dulled light coming in from the alley. Its head was Styrofoam like you buy in a fabric store, eyeless and robotic.

Because of where I sat I saw the kid right away when he came in. But he didn't see me, or pretended not to. He sat down at the counter with a cup of coffee and yesterday's paper. I could tell it was yesterday's because of the picture on the front page of one of the fires southeast by Anaconda. He had his back to me. Tattoo behind his left ear just visible. There were a couple of smaller photos underneath, at the bottom of the page—smoke jumpers who'd been burned alive.

I looked down at my book but didn't see anything. If he was pretending not to notice me, I'd be able to tell. There'd be a *thing* going on between us. I didn't feel anything. I was sorry I hadn't given him a ride. But he could've stayed and done something about the baby, about the other Ruth. And now she was dead. The air conditioning was broken. Me all damp and itchy with the heat. Maybe he felt me watching him then because he turned. I looked back at my book.

I was trying to think of what to do but then he stood up fast with this *look*. Angry and then, relieved. He'd *have* to see me now. But he didn't. He just walked out of there fast. The skinny kid behind the counter put a bagel down where he'd been sitting, the coffee cup still full. I was looking up, so when he talked it was to me.

Did he just leave?

I shrugged and looked around. That's when I saw her. Crystal standing in line with her baby wrapped in a knit blue blanket. She had her dirty blond dreads draped over it and she was whispering. She lifted her face, her eyes all smudged in black and when she saw me she smiled. I didn't want to look at her. I didn't want to talk to her. Maybe she'd know I'd left that thing by the side of the party house with a good-as-dead girl. Left it like a stray. I couldn't think of what a real mamma would do or say to me about a thing like that. Crystal wouldn't say anything, which would be worse.

My book shut and I stood to finish my coffee like I was rushed. I got my purse and didn't look up again to where she stood and watched me run. I turned to go, rifling in my purse like I was looking for something and pushed through the swinging back door to the alley. It was scorching even in this forever twilight, the fake wind the wildfires had fattened blew two plastic bags bloated and aloft, down the alley and toward the empty street. I ran my fingers through my hair and put my shades on for sun-smoke or spiritual pestilence protection and squinted both ways but he was gone.

TWENTY-ONE

I ordered a vodka gimlet. The James Bar had faux log cabin décor like every other bar in town with fake timber-frame supports tacked to the ceiling. But there everything was polyurethaned to a thick gloss intended, I supposed, to turn the log-cabin look chic. Bridget ordered a glass of dolcetto, which was brownish or maroon like dried blood. When I left Butterfly Herbs I'd called her, and she'd said we should meet up there, since it was between her place and mine. We sat at a small table in the corner against some mirrors. She wore a pale-green backless dress in t-shirt material that fit her perfectly and had one arm perched on the tabletop. The wine had stained her lips and teeth and her eyes were bloodshot, maybe from the smoke. She grinned at her reflection and rubbed at the fronts of her teeth with her finger.

God my mouth's all. Like a vampire.

She took another drink, glanced at her phone on the table, got out some lip gloss.

It's the right color, I said and swallowed.

She opened her mouth a little and tilted her face up slightly to gloss her lips, her eyes on herself in the mirror. She smiled and checked her phone.

I finished my drink and shook the ice.

What?

Nothing. Just earlier I saw Crystal. She's like. A witch or something.

Witch? She's just high is all.

I shook the ice in my glass a little more, stared hard at the wet cubes.

You know what I heard? she said. Red foods are like, really good for you.

So, I said. But it was better to just play along. I sighed. What, like beets?

Yeah beets, red wine, strawberries, red meat.

Blood.

Some cultures drink blood.

What, like vampires, zombies?

Seriously. I saw it on National Geographic HD, she said. They actually seemed totally healthy. Good skin, straight white teeth.

Yeah, like vampires.

You want to eat here or someplace else?

I'd rather drink than eat, I said.

She was acting like everything was normal, and so was I, drinking a cocktail like always. She took the menu off the table next to us where a couple sat each ignoring the other, loathing the other, dragging it out for the struggle, for the fight. What was the point? To torture yourself for nothing. I wasn't doing much better but still I thought I'd rather be dead than be like that.

What if they weren't done with that? I said.

The menu didn't matter, the couple didn't care but it was something to say. The boyfriend looked like he was ready to kill somebody. His eyes. Open too wide, crazed, on fire with his eyebrows up. His body calm except for his fingers, tapping hard on the table, his jaw clenching and unclenching. I looked where he was but didn't see anything. His girl was sending a text.

Oh come on, they weren't using it.

She was right, they hadn't even noticed, and she started to read aloud.

Seasoned fries, crab cakes, portabella mushroom sandwich, boring, sliders. *Slider?* Sounds like the shits.

I laughed. The waitress was standing over our table. She set another drink by me even though I hadn't ordered it, which was cool. I didn't want her to think I was laughing at *her*, but it was a relief to smile a little. Bridget smirked. It might've seemed like I was another bitch. I tried to look her meaningfully in the eye but she didn't see.

It's a miniature burger, the waitress said, smiling so hard she grimaced. You've had White Castle, right?

Bridget gave her the once-over. She wasn't bad-looking but her clothes were cheap.

Okay, Bridget said. Do the *sliders* come with anything?

I felt sorry for the waitress with her rayon pants, trying to hide a wad of kryptonite gum in her cheek. She looked exhausted, depressed. She looked like how I felt. Maybe she went to the parties. Or maybe her boyfriend liked to shove her around. I hadn't meant to laugh.

Home fries mixed greens or slaw. She said it as fast like it was one thing, homefriesmixgreensorslaw.

Slaw?

Bridget sniffed.

Why don't you come back in like, five minutes?

The waitress gave Bridget the once-over, chewed her gum a couple times, and left. She hadn't looked at me at all.

You can be a real bitch, I said pretending to laugh but I meant it.

Oh come on, you know she thinks *slider* sounds nasty. She's just pissed because she has to act like she's crazy about them. I mean, she's probably a vegetarian.

You were a vegetarian.

That was like forever ago.

Her glass was almost empty with red silt at the bottom. The waitress hadn't brought *her* another. But she didn't seem to notice.

I'll leave her a big tip, she said. It'll make her night.

Our drinks would be about fifteen bucks and she dropped a twenty on the table.

Let's get out of here, she said.

Outside ash fell softly like snow. But since it was nearly full night, the wind had died. We walked through downtown, past the pawnshops with rifles and pistols in the windows, past the Annual Pig Roast behind the Old Post Pub. There were a bunch of people there and the music was loud, everybody with a half-finished drink. Bridget stopped to watch the pig crisp and slowly turn. I stood watching her from behind. She must've felt it; she turned quickly and looked me up and down before I had the chance to look away. A cop drove by, turning to stare as he passed. We pretended not to notice, didn't talk about it. Bridget's legs were already perfect but looked longer and thinner than usual. She had on BGBG Girls Gladiator sandals in black alligator skin. I wished they were mine, but without her employee discount I could never afford them. Her purse matched: a little clutch in black alligator with spikes on the strap around her wrist. A touch of punk.

We wound up at one of the bistros that pretended it was in Seattle or Portland but didn't quite get it right. Our waiter wore an oversized tie in bright nineties colors. He pretended he had the specials memorized but he didn't. He gave me a snarly smile and winked.

Bridget ignored him and when he was done talking she ordered a bottle of red wine, the beet appetizer and steak. She didn't look up.

Beets? I said when he'd left.

You can't care, do you, Ruth? It's healthy, she said. It's on me anyway.

Technically, Bridget owed me money, a couple hundred bucks. But I wouldn't ask her for it, not even now. It was better this way, to keep the balance. Anyway, she had like three credit cards, almost maxed. She'd pay one off with the other. If I hadn't been near the end of my money, maybe I'd have paid for everything so I wouldn't owe her anything, so I could leave anytime. But as it was, I was stuck. I'd have to do what she wanted.

You all right? I said.

God I can't wait for that steak. She checked her phone. She smiled weakly at me.

George had told me that when I was a baby and a little kid, he loved me best when I was sick. I was so small and helpless. And without a mother, he had this fear the littlest things would kill me. Influenza, the common cold, ear infections. That's what I felt for Bridget then. Pity.

Tell me something exciting, Ruth.

She leaned back in her chair and rested her bleached head on her hand. There was so much we could've said, needed to be said, but we were miles apart. The words when she spoke them didn't say what they would've had they been spoken by me. Maybe that was what kept us friends. We heard what we wanted, no matter what the other meant. That is, we had an understanding, we weren't friends for nothing. Maybe I'd been too hard on her lately. Maybe it really had gotten to her, whatever it really meant that Lydia and Audrey had come back around, and the parties over, someone she'd known forever dead.

She glanced at the bar. Where is our wine?

Like what?

What do you mean *like what*, she said and flicked her fingers at me. I just want my fucking wine.

Jesus, Bridget, I mean what do you want me to tell you about if you want something so exciting; why don't you just tell me what?

Oh I don't know. What were you doing all week?

She was looking at the bar. I decided to be honest, or what I wished was honest.

Like writing.

The wine came, and the waiter's prunish hands uncorked the bottle with a stupid flourish. He watched us. Bridget did something with her phone. Maybe it was a boy. Or maybe it was Lydia. You never knew exactly.

Oh yeah? she said.

She tasted the drop of wine. Her teeth touched in something like a snarl. Her eye upon me. The waiter poured. I didn't understand her. I didn't understand why we were friends in the first place. Sometimes it was like she didn't know the first thing about me. If she did, if she knew what a freak I was, she wouldn't be sitting here. Or maybe she did have some idea, and it was something she could wear. Like the spikes on her clutch, a touch of punk.

What were you *writing?* She might not have realized she'd said it like an insult.

What do you think?

She knew I wrote poems, or tried to. We'd taken poetry together, it's where we met. Which had ruined it for me because with her watching I couldn't write anything at all. I tasted the wine. It was a thick purplish red and it tasted slightly metallic. But then again, she probably wanted to insult me. We drank and the food arrived, the steak oozing a watery blood.

Rare, I said.

Don't lie, Ruth, she said. You were going crazy in there. You were just drunk.

TWENTY-TWO

It was one of those nights where the whole town was drunk. And so I was, stepping diagonally across the sidewalk tugging at my yellow dress and staring. The fires getting closer all the time; I'd be out of money soon. We passed the Oxford. Inside the filthy windows the 24-hour poker game was getting started. Maybe I could learn to gamble. It was a rough crowd around the table, unshaven, sunken, ravenous eyes, yellowing skin and stubble. The skinny dealer looked up from his deck when we passed but he didn't smile. Folds of sour skin around his little mouth, yellow fingers. And a couple too-clean guys stood on the corner out front, shouting with an inch between them like they were going to kiss.

My fucking sister was raped by a nigger man, and you want to tell me what?

I'm very sorry about that, I'm very sorry to hear that, but that doesn't mean.

And you want me to just go ahead and like every nigger I see?

This is America, I thought. It doesn't stop. They say God. Bless. When you sneeze, they say that. Invisible They. Invisible white us. Some of us.

I'm just saying, man, you can't judge the whole bushel by one rotten apple.

I've heard that before.

I have lots of African American friends. And you really shouldn't say that kind of. Kind of shit. Man.

He said African American like he was saying Negro. Like this was what it was, temporal regression.

You think my sister getting raped is just some bullshit? I'll fucking kill those niggers. You hear me, man, I will fucking kill them.

I stuck to the other side of the sidewalk, close to the parking meters, and ashed my Camel into the gutter. Bridget walked curled over her phone, sending a text. The screen cast a rectangle of bluish light on the middle of her face. We were almost to Charlie's when she stopped and looked up.

Shit, there's that dance party at the Badlander, Bridget said. Lydia texted me.

I stopped and gave her a look but she didn't see, she was looking at her phone.

I almost forgot what day it is. We were supposed to meet up.

In certain situations, it helped to have a little buzz on. To keep you honest.

Well I'll see you later then? I said.

Oh come on, Ruth, you can *come.* I mean, it's a bar. Anybody can come.

I made a noise like a snort and shook my head. Maybe there'd be a cover. I didn't want to pay a cover.

I just mean, she said. I just mean. They said they have some kind of plan about the parties and that I can help. So we were gonna like, hang out and make a plan.

No it's cool. You know. I just get bored watching you. You and them.

You don't *really* care, do you? I mean, you're not even *from* here.

Of course I care, Bridget, come on, I said. You're like, my best friend.

I regretted it as soon as I said it. Bridget smiled and dropped her phone into her clutch, making a show of giving me her full attention. We were standing in front of this bad sushi joint with one-way mirrors for a storefront. My eyes burned and watered, which made me angry for how it must look—as *if* I'd cry right now. I checked my yellow dress, my hair. It looked better now that it was dry from the fiery air, like beach hair. Bridget turned and gave herself the once over. She looked at the reflection of my wet bloodshot eyes and started to talk. Which was so stupid, I looked away from her in the mirror to the side of her real face, still watching mine in reflection. She was so fucking pretty. I wanted to touch her so I got out my smokes, my shades, put them on, lit one, took my shades off again. It was stupid to wear sunglasses at night.

Well then you'll get where I'm coming from, she said to my reflection, her voice all slippery. I can't even begin to tell you how hard it's been for me. I mean, I've know those girls since I can remember. Since like the second grade.

I thought they were like, horrible back then, I said. I thought you weren't even friends until like senior year.

She'd told me all about elementary school. Like how they'd locked her in the janitor's closet so long that she'd wet herself. But when she told me the story originally, she could've been lying.

Horrible? she said. I mean, we were *kids*. Kids are always horrible. But in any case, you weren't even there. You can't know what happened.

Yeah. Kids.

Maybe that was some kind of reference to the baby at the party. In which case she was right. I didn't know what had happened. I'd walked away.

Anyway, she said they have an idea about the parties, like something like an End of the World Party since God it's like the fucking apocalypse around here. But they said they need my help to pull it off.

She smiled.

I thought they shut it all down, I said. I thought the cops stopped the parties for good.

She laughed.

You think the cops can do anything? God the cops aren't in charge, Ruth, it's the Internet and like, credit cards. But anyway, Lydia and Audrey said the hosts were thinking maybe it was better. Like they were sick of hosting all the time. So this will be different. It'll be at my place was what they were thinking.

So Bridget was theirs and I was nobody's. So they'd unite against me now, to make themselves what they always could've become. Unless she'd been theirs all along. Or maybe the other Ruth was my fault. I didn't know. I was drunk. I didn't know anything. I didn't know what was going on around me.

We talked about it, she said. And they've just like, had so much going on and everything. But now.

She didn't really look like she was lying. In which case, she should've known that was bullshit. She should've known they were using her. Maybe.

Look, she said. We relate on this like other level, you and me. I really like that about our friendship, Ruth, seriously. But we just don't have the same *history* as with those girls. It's a difference, that's all.

I supposed I'd always hated her.

Yeah, she said. Those girls, they're not fake. They won't act like they like you if they don't. But that doesn't make them bad people.

She glanced in the direction we'd come, toward the Badlander.

Come on, Ruth, she said. It'll be fun.

Bridget, I said to the back of her head.

She waited, looking at me almost patiently, but I had nothing to say.

I was pathetic. Pathetic to watch like a little bitch from the side. Lay down. Roll over. Shake. I should've told her, but I was thinking in every direction at once and there weren't any words for that. I should've said fine then I was going home, but I only stood there not doing anything. Her phone rang in her clutch. She took it out and looked at me and frowned.

I thought you'd be happy for me, Ruth. She flipped her phone on and smiled into the blue light.

Anyway, I said. I seriously don't want to pass those assholes again.

Which assholes? she said.

She'd gotten a tiny pink wand out and leaned toward the one-way mirrors with her mouth open. She picked a bit of ash from the tip and glossed her lips. There might've been people eating dinner on the other side, people watching us.

Oh, those two are probably like besties by now.

Seriously? I said. They were like this close to a fucking fight.

I got out a compact and checked my makeup like a normal person. She couldn't help but look me up and down then, assessing.

This is Montana, Ruth, she said. They don't have anything to fight about. Oh don't look like *that*, Ruth, you're prettier than *that*.

She laughed and reached her hand to my face and with two fingers shoved my mouth roughly into something like a smile. My heart burned, choking me.

I mean we're still *friends*, she said. We'll *always* be friends. Give me a hug.

She embraced me weirdly without getting too close. I was small and filthy touching her, grazing the edge of the florescent light coming off her.

Come on, Ruth, it'll be fun, she said. You're not worried about your *outfit* are you? Your dress is like, totally *you*. Plus it'll be so crowded they won't even notice.

She started walking again. I had some trouble with my lighter but I followed, keeping just behind her.

TWENTY-THREE

Motherfucker motherfucker, is what this asshole slurred. The tent hissed. But it was the smoke and air knocked out of my lungs that woke me. It was as if my ribs broke, crushing my lungs' soft red insides. I rasped, gasped, dragged out of the fallen tent and looked up. Big hobo swaying. It was Bong, Lurch's man. He staggered once. I opened my mouth to speak but couldn't get enough air to shove a word out. In the shadows just behind him, Ben paced smoking a butt, talking to himself and not looking at Bong or me, as if nothing was happening at all.

Hey. Man, I managed.

I didn't know if I meant Ben, if I was asking for help, or if I meant Bong. In my sleeping bag like a Gore-Tex worm. Bong grinned and flicked his one dread back when he raised his boot. It wasn't just the smile. In his putrid, shit-brown eyes all bloodshot from the smoke I could see he liked this. He liked this. When the boot hit my stomach I curled robotically. I did not have feeling or thought, I was a man-machine. The me in me was gone, long gone and the night a black halo around his skull. He moved slow, but he'd caught me off guard, knocked the wind out of me again. I tried to rip my sleeping bag open by the zipper, tried to worm my way out.

You think you punk, motherfucker? he said. Where's it at?

The boot in my face now, the smell the taste of my skull and blood. A whiteness, filled my eyes and mind. I must've fainted.

Dumpster rat? he was saying. Nice bag. You got more? You got more?

He meant the sleeping bag, I thought. Unless he knew and meant my cash.

I mean, I ask myself, he said. What kind of crusty travels with that much cash?

The boot, softer this time, and something spacious and light hit my shoulder, a liquor bottle shattered, the sound high-pitched.

He'd aimed for my head and missed. I could hear Ben muttering from somewhere, but I couldn't tell what he was saying. Around us the air was all slurred hisses and glass bottle clinks and trash bag rustlings with drunks fucking wrapped up in them.

I got some air back. Fuck you.

Then nothing.

I got myself to standing, the world with the spins. Blood from my nostrils, blood in my eyes, my tongue. And the asshole crouched there with his hands on his knees and his head down, his one dreadlock over his shoulder. Panting like he was waiting, just waiting for me to destroy him. Lucky for me he was drunk as that, thinking double, didn't have the sense to look for the money before he laid into me. Dumpster Rat. Throwaway kid. Dumb shit. I grabbed the good as empty Karkov bottle from the wet grass.

You want what? I said.

And swung it down hard, right where his left ear met his throat and skull. It didn't break. He didn't look up before he fell, in slow motion. He lay in the grass with blood in his shut eye and it's no lie that asshole was smiling. From a ways off some hidden kid's voice slurred, Hey asshole. And Ben muttered, paced, glanced in my direction again and again but the snitch didn't dare get any closer.

I held my fingers beneath Bong's nostrils to feel his breath, stuffed five bucks in his pocket. I don't know why I did it exactly, a fuck-you or maybe it was pity. In my tent I rifled around in the bottom of my pack and finally felt the pistol. I stuck it in the back of my belt, I'd have to keep it with me always now. The cash was there, it was, all of it. I peeled a couple hundred bucks from one bankroll. I'd get a cheap room. And then I'd find someplace to crash. So I left the tent as-is and Ben muttering in the dark, took off toward town, always glancing behind me at the teeming night in Hellgate.

TWENTY-FOUR

The Badlander was packed when we got inside. A room filled with bodies, smoke-smell strong but the air not thick with it but damp with sweat. Half-nude, skins glistening in oily bolts across the room. It was the DJ from the party up on stage wiping his nose intermittently and rocking to the beat. His girl was there with her camera. He pumped his open hand at the air and when he paused she took his picture, then pointed the camera at the crowd. These drunk girls in the front waved their hands at her to take theirs but she ignored them. The bass heaved, the mob squirmed. The girls in the front screeched intoxicatedly. Bridget raised her eyebrows at me excitedly, scanned the room with her phone lit blue in her hand. I didn't see Lydia or Audrey and I didn't want to. What was the point? Bridget's bleached hair shone red in the bar lights. I leaned toward her and shouted into her ear.

I've got to pee, I'll come find you.

She dug her pearly-white nails into my arm. Don't sneak off on me, Ruth.

I shook my head.

I needed a drink. The bathroom door had no lock, and there were a couple girls inside making out but they didn't look up. The shorter one wore a blue shirtdress that was pulled beneath her bare left breast. Her chest was covered in scratches. The other girl had trendy bleached and blackened hair but I couldn't see her face, just the glint of her bleached teeth. I shut the door. The song changed, it was MIA. Missing in Action.

I wiped my face, I was already sweating. I didn't see Bridget anymore and it was a relief to be free of her even for one fucking minute. Boys crowded, bellied up to the bar two or three deep and a couple of them stepped aside to make room for me so I leaned against it with my cash in my hand. I was running low. But then again, Bridget was my friend, which meant no matter how much I hated her, or wanted just to be rid of her for good, there was supposed to be love between us.

The bartenders moved rhythmically, in time with M.I.A. who said, I'm knocking on the doors of your Hummer Hummer. Yeah I'm knocking on the doors of your Hummer Hummer. Yeah we're hungry like the wolves hunting dinner dinner.

Vodka soda, I said. Double. Lime.

I enjoyed ordering well. I looked around like I had someone I was with. Which was what being friends with Bridget was all about, having someone to look around for at the bar, at the party, make you seem legitimate. Otherwise you're just standing alone, a loser, a nobody. And it was best if that someone wasn't just anybody. It was best if that somebody was good-looking, was cool like Bridget, which is to say that even now I needed her.

So that more than I hated Bridget, I hated my stupid fucking self. Just a freak alone. A nobody, a nothing. Like I was the void all this shit was spinning around. Like maybe this was all just my dream, my nightmare. Apartment filthy, no man, job, no nothing now or ever but drunk.

I thought I'd cry but I didn't. I finished my drink. I didn't see Bridget or Lydia or Audrey. And I wasn't going to stand there alone like an asshole. But then I did see them. Or I didn't see, but I knew. A space in the crowd cleared. The girl onstage with the camera still but nobody was trying to get her to shoot, they were watching something in that clearing. I caught sight of Bridget's bleached head. She waded her way through the stands of swaying bodies and when she reached the clearing she flipped her hair and said hello. After a moment she shrugged and looked up, scanning the bar for me. I turned away. Before I could do this, or anything, I needed a smoke.

TWENTY-FIVE

Maybe I was scared. Maybe Bong's crusty piece of shit friends were trailing me and I didn't know it. Bunch of white trash angry ass motherfuckers, probably they can smell fear, like dogs. And to think I figured it'd be Dick who'd come for the money. Funny. Ha ha. I would've laughed, but the pain was starting in my skull. Blood in my swelling shut eye. But anyway I couldn't see the moon or the mountain shapes lit up by it behind the smoke.

At the rapids the waters rushed deafeningly. I stopped panting to catch my breath and looked back, but there was nobody. My triceps against the synthetic pack, the pistol heavy at my back. I pulled it out. Heavy long-barreled six-shooter. The Preacher's Gun. It was warm, dampish with sweat. It caught the moonlight, heavy in my hand. Some line I remembered. Something like, 32-20 I'm gonna shoot my gal and run. I'd shot it before. I aimed up the trail. So what, now every fucking hobo would know or did know I had a stash of cash. And if one of them could stay sober or sane long enough they'd off me and take it. But I had the gun. To shoot it I had to take the safety off. I tried that. Just a little move of the thumb. The trigger the same. A flick and you're dead. Don't get caught.

When a stick broke in the woods I stuck the gun back in my belt and kept on not looking side to side like some weenie kid. I wasn't afraid. I wasn't afraid. I was walking thinking, Shitbag nobody motherfuckers they were nothing to me they had nothing on me I'd kill those motherfuckers kill them. From now on I'd have that gun all the time and if they tried to take what I'd taken, pow. But there was something in the trail that made me stop. Something thin and small and dark, like nothing really. A picture, a photograph. I knelt to pick it up. Pops in the river and his Wranglers and no shirt. Somebody was fucking with me. Somebody was *fucking* with me. Probably they were watching me right now. Right. Now. I ran.

The weak city lights bleeding into the pale night-smoke over-head illumined the trail somewhat so I could see what the next photo was before I picked it up. My mom in a crimson dress. And the next and the next, I snatched them as I ran, not looking side to side not stopping to breathe even in town under the streetlights I ran. Past the pawnshops and apartments, past the barbershops, the banks, past the 24-hour poker game, the bars, the casinos. Didn't stop until the first motel I saw, all strung up in pink lights.

You could die, you could die, don't get caught.

Just like that I'm standing this side of the courtesy counter, the graveyard desk clerk's television flashing through the big fish tank that made up part of the wall. Paying for a room's like bleeding money, and without money, I'm done. So I rub my skull blinking, thinking. Photos in my hand. I have no choice. For a couple nights I can swing it. Then dig up some place to crash. Some hippie house, or some girl. Girls are easy.

All the while I'm thinking how I'm in this little lit up glass box just like that fish. And the clerk doesn't show and doesn't show, so I start ringing the bell over and over and over. And whoever's watching in the dark on the other side of the glass, and me with my pack full of cash, with my photos they stole and gave back. But why? Like I'm volunteering, Come on in and shoot me! But they don't, they won't. They'd rather fuck with me first. I wanted a drink, needed a drink; I needed a place to hide.

So I start saying, Hey, Hey. Loud. And I'm sweating, the gun tip a cold cock caressing the top of my ass crack. With them watching me. Watching me. So I stuff those photos in some cellphone-specific zippered pocket on the side of my pack, and in my mind I'm all, I do not know how to use this gun. I do not know how to use this gun.

At last the clerk comes with her hair a-tussle and her hands in the air like this is a stick-up until she sees me. Then she puts on her bitch face and says, Yes? She's got sleep lines and mascara bleeding all around her squint-eyes but I just say, Room please. And she says, And how are you going to pay for that then? and I say, Cash.

TWENTY-SIX

Outside I smoothed my dress and got my smokes out. Some old bums loitered on the sidewalk sharing a bottle of Karkov Vodka. The way they drained it should've made me sick. One hobo with long stringy hair and a stray eye stumbled up to me. Lou Reed against the wall there; she didn't give a shit about traffic today.

Scuse me, ma'am. Scuse me. You got some extra change for us all? Jus like thirty-seven cents it's all we looking for.

I started to feel around in my purse. Which was stupid. I was broke too.

Reuben man, you've got to try someplace *else* man, this was a man's voice slightly slurred, coming from just behind me. You've totally like saturated this area, you know? You're not going to get anything keep asking the same people. It's simple economics is what it is, man.

Fuck you, the hobo said.

I turned. It was the traveler kid from the party. He stepped back. The side of his face all swollen, his lip busted, his eye red turning black like smoke off a fire. He swallowed and looked around.

I'm not trying to fuck with you, Reuben. He rubbed his skull. He touched the small of his back with one hand. Here have a buck, have two, I don't give a fuck, I'm just trying to say. I'm just trying to give you a little friendly advice is all.

He knew the hobo's name. The bucks he pulled all wrinkled

from his pocket. The hobo didn't refuse, looked at the kid for a while with his good eye like he'd killed or spat on him. He staggered to where Lou Reed sat and stood wavering like flames, like grasses, the dollars loose in his hand. He took the bottle and drank. The kid shook his head.

Probably already forgot what I said, he said. I'm James. He took my hand. So where do I know you from?

Ruth, I said again. We met. At the party. And it's my friend you recognize. Remember?

Right, he said. Right.

When he smiled his lip oozed. He got out a pouch of tobacco, glanced at the hobos and rolled a cigarette.

But it's you I liked, he said. And glanced up at me with his feverish eyes like lit glass. Smoke these? he said. He handed me a perfect rollie. A deep red slash across the palm of his hand.

What? I said.

We're speaking the same language, he said. He glanced at the hobos again. Look, let me buy you a drink, he said.

I just. I shrugged. I didn't stare at his face. Here? I said.

I got to get off this corner, he said. There's time to make it someplace, it's like two hours before last call.

I don't know, I said. I mean I just got here. I trailed off, looking at the door. I shouldn't leave Bridget. She'd be pissed. She'd bought me dinner. Drinks. And if I stuck around, maybe it'd end up cool with Lydia and Audrey. Whereas if I left, there'd be no chance. He sparked his lighter. His face was a mess. I'd seen bar fights before. There was something about it I liked. In the doorway a bouncer with his arms crossed, chewing this kryptonite gum. James lit my cigarette and I inhaled, drew it from between my lips.

I just, I said and exhaled. I had to step outside. I don't know. I can't leave really.

Past the bouncer the edge of the crowd, hands in the air licked the ceiling like brush-fire flames. James checked the hobos, but they didn't look back.

My Bridget, I said. I mean my *friend* Bridget, it was her idea to come here anyway and it's just.

I'm not going in there, James said. That Monroe? He stared at the open door for a long time then.

I don't know, I said. She just. Who?

She'd be pissed if you leave, he nodded.

She might not even notice, I said.

Have her meet up with you, he said. It's not like I'm kidnapping you. He started walking, hands in his pockets, looking around him as he went. I don't know why but I followed, sending Bridget a text. Like I *had* to follow. Like maybe he would get me out of this alive. I glanced back, half expecting Bridget running after me. Then we were around the corner, The Golden Rose Liquor Lounge and Casino with its sign hung behind some filthy bullet-proof glass, and beside it the store-front Evangelical church. *Prepare.* But inside it was empty, dark.

Here? I said.

How about someplace else. Farther. I mean you're from here, right? Take me someplace. Someplace quiet. Someplace where we can talk, like someplace real.

A cop driving in the other direction made a U-turn and drove slow past us, staring. I put my head down, my hands in my pockets. James kept walking acting like he didn't notice and flicked the cherry from his cigarette. The butt he rolled between his thumb and fingers, scattering the tobacco like an offering.

I don't know why I followed. Like I didn't have a choice. His hair and brow were dark. His eyes feverish and half-wild, bloodshot like everybody else. I hoped I looked all right, pulled at the armholes of my dress. We turned left on Higgins. I tried to think of something to say but couldn't. There wasn't anybody outside the Oxford, everybody was inside gambling, everybody was at poker.

You got a place in mind then?

Not in mind I guess, just my bar. I've been trying to get back there all night. It's usually quiet. Early at least.

At Charlie's I pulled the door open. It was busy for a Thursday. Everybody fleeing the smoke indoors. James was scanning the room like there might be somebody he was trying to avoid. Which I could understand, that's how it is in a small town. Near the door sat some regulars who looked up and nodded when I came in. Some cooks drinking Bloody Marys after work, old-timers, and skinny twins who made a living digging up crystals in the woods. They sat at a high table with one bottle of Budweiser between them and their hands like dirty claws. On the table they had a huge crystal and they sat staring at it. James ordered whiskeys and watched the television while they were poured. He got out a twenty, his wallet filled with cash. It was local news, footage of home-owners fleeing, as close as Florence, as close as Turah. His hand shook when he reached for his glass. He pushed a drink toward me.

I didn't know what to say so I drank. His face was pretty bad. But I wouldn't ask. It was too predictable to ask. He gazed at his cigarette in the ashtray and glanced at me hard from the bright sides of his eyes. I could smell him. Thick and hoarse and faintly sweet. Booze and sweat and smoke and leather. A hobo smell, with wildfire. Unlike Bridget's smell, which was easy to explain. Flowers, citrus. Or Lydia's, which was prim. John Lee Hooker on the radio. I smiled at my drink.

It was cool he'd been at the party. Maybe he'd even gotten an invitation. Bridget hadn't sent a text back or called. He stared at the bar top and I breathed the air stuck to him. Then we both talked at once.

Do you wear cologne?

So how long you lived here anyway? he said.

We laughed. I was just trying to think of something to say but it had come off stupid. I wished I'd kept my mouth shut. I shrugged, blushing. The bartender I recognized from the parties put another round on the bar without us asking. He sipped and winced, in pain or like someone who disliked drinking liquor and had done a lot of it.

It was a gift, he said. From my stepfather. The cologne.

Yeah.

He looked at one of my eyes, the other. I could see that he was drunk, that there was something he wanted, but anyway I forgot about the bar. It was as if I'd known him in another country. He touched his temple. I followed his long fingers to the Evil Eye, tattooed behind his ear. I'd seen that tattoo before.

My dad's dead, he said. He died here. In Montana.

I nodded.

He was a good man, he said. Unless he wasn't.

Is that why you're here? In Missoula?

Yeah just to see what I could find out. And I've been hearing all kinds of craziness about my pops since I arrived. That he had another kid, that somebody killed him.

That's rough, I said. My mom's dead, but it was cancer that killed her.

Until then, Bridget was the only other person I knew whose mom or dad was dead. Bridget's mom liked to say somebody killed *her* dad too, but that was just an excuse. So she could sit around watching TV all day feeling sorry for herself.

I could've told him about it, but I didn't. I didn't have to talk about Bridget if I didn't want to.

Just before last call the place filled, everybody spilling their drinks. It made James nervous, he'd start every time somebody brushed up against him. Which was over and over because people were packed in there—under the black and white photographs of the old regulars that covered the walls, by the pool table, around the slot machines. I recognized some guests from the parties but nobody said hello. The loud liquoured talk and the click of glass on glass or on the bar muffled us so that what wasn't whispered was a shout.

Somebody turned the music up. Now we all tied up and my life is ruined, Sonny Boy sang. I'm scared of that child, he sang, I'm scared of that child, I'm too young to die. James ordered another round. He watched the room steadily, keeping everything in his sights and all the while he smoked. He was dressed in military surplus with a worn gray-blue t-shirt and a cap but his black boots looked expensive, some kind of soft-looking leather with a smoothly curved toe and an Italian word stamped into the sole.

When the crowd started to thin again he quit scanning and turned to watch the televisions where the news was on. It was the usual hooded prisoners in orange, and soldiers. The picture was blurry, taken through thick razor-wire coils from outside the prison's fences. Then it was back to the blonde newscaster. Helicopters, desert, some young man with his nose and mouth covered who threw a bomb at us watching through the camera's eye. The blonde pivoted her chair stretching her plastic mouth and the next frame was red carpet, paparazzi, flash bulbs exploding. James shook his head once.

Crazy how they do that, he said. Torture facility, warfare as if it's just the same as some zombie in Louis Vuitton. That's why I figured, I'd make like my pops did, get to a place like Montana, leave the bullshit behind. Like retrace his steps.

Yeah, I said. You showed up just in time to see it all go down. See it all burn. I meant my laugh to come off bitter. I drank. To watch it all get just completely fucked. There wasn't any reason to be angry, I told myself. Because what was the point? I swallowed. I tried to count how many drinks I'd had since the night started. I stopped at six or seven. I was getting soberer all the time. I was like a fucking nun over here.

Yeah, he said. Or me. I mean look at my face. *Look* at it.

Your face is fucked, I said.

We both laughed.

If I told you, you wouldn't believe it, he said. It's like. I should just turn around right now, go back to Minneapolis and get a job at Target Headquarters or something. Just forget about it. He's not even my father really. I didn't know until a couple weeks ago, so what's the point? But now I'm here. I don't have a choice anymore. I just have to. Keep going. You know?

I didn't, but I nodded anyway, all serious and not looking at him. He coughed.

Anyway, he said. I've heard people say Fire Season. But this. You can't see across the fucking street. Forget about mountains. It's like. The apocalypse.

This *is* the apocalypse, I said. Basically.

It was stupid to talk like that. Go Green or Prepare. Melodramatic, as if I really believed. Nothing was coming to an end. Nothing would change.

That girl from the party is dead you know, I said.

Which girl?

The one all passed out outside, I said. And there was that. That. With her.

I couldn't say baby. It was embarrassing. Like saying Revolution or I love you.

Dead? he said.

The police tried to stop them, I said. But they can't. Nobody can. I *wish* they would. I hate the parties. I wouldn't go if I could. I mean, that girl is *dead*. Her name was Ruth. Maybe it's like, a sign. Maybe they're trying to tell me something. Like I'm next.

I stopped. I was talking drunk. The bar was full of guests from the parties.

I shouldn't say that, I said.

Someone was always listening.

I mean, I *like* the parties, I said a little louder. It's just like. In the morning? I can't like remember half of it.

I pretended to laugh like I thought it was fun and pretended to drink again, but my drink was gone. Somebody was always listening. People looked at us some of the time. Looked at his busted face. I rubbed my own face. I was exhausted. I wished he wouldn't look at me. I would cry, I thought I would cry.

You want to get out of here? he said.

I shrugged. We just got here. I mean if you want to stay. It's been a long night.

It was almost last call and Bridget hadn't sent a text back. Which was bad, like in the end she didn't give a shit if I left or not. I got out a cigarette. James lit it and stood up. It was funny how he knew I had to leave, but that didn't mean anything. Around us drunks leaned on their palms against the bar or with feet apart for balance, dead-eyeing the flashing, digitized slot machines. There were casinos everywhere in this town. The bartenders were about to turn the lights up.

So, you from here? he said.

Minneapolis, I said. Bloomington actually. Here nobody knows the difference.

That's it, he said. I *told you* I recognized you. From around probably. Ah Bloomington. Home to the Mall of America. You must be proud. I'm from the city. South side. Mall of America was my mall.

My mall. It helped, somehow. Like now I knew he was safe. He put out his hand for me to go, and I turned and started for the door with him behind like a gentleman or something. Outside a couple clear-eyed, dead-sober Flathead or maybe Blackfoot Indians stood against the brick wall watching some more white boys stumble past. Beneath a busted shopping cart across the street some hobos passed out.

Hung out on the West Bank mainly, James said. Hard Times, the 400, Nomad. That whole scene. Punk scene. Old hobos, random refugee types, dealers. That where I'd have seen you?

I shrugged. I wished he'd known me from the West Bank, but that wasn't it. Whenever I'd be over there for a show, the kids that hung around in front of Hard Times all tattoos with their homemade bikes, they just knew I wasn't one of them. Like how I knew James wasn't really one of them, was just pretending. But it didn't matter.

TWENTY-SEVEN

Under the town lights, the night sky was a shit-brown. We walked by the tracks watching the still train cars and the humps of the dry hills behind. The dry grasses tinder waiting for a spark. Then a train approached, its hollow whistle unfastened from the machine. Its whistle on the bitter, smoked night air over the river water slipping past us on its bank, over the empty streets. James took long, labored steps and frowned and smoked in the smoke. We'd walked for a long time, mostly not talking before we stood before the Bel Aire Motel rimmed in sinister pink florescent lights. Lighting icing, or the filling in Motel Cake.

Ah, he said. That's funny I've got a room here.

Which was some bullshit but did I care? He looked in every direction like he was trying to get his bearings.

Yeah? I said. What a. Coincidence.

Didn't even realize, he said. We were close.

He grinned that I could fuck you grin but maybe I'd imagined it. Maybe I didn't mind. I didn't mind. We started to walk again, past the Bel Aire pool, chlorinic, encased in a glass cage. I'd go inside with him, I could go in with him, it didn't make a difference. If it was me he wanted or if this all was just to get something. We passed the front office where a sallow, fat girl sat behind the desk watching television. Nobody stood in the pink and moon light on the wrap-around balconies in front of their room smoking a cigarette or watching us. He didn't take my hand but he could've.

And he didn't hold the door. He entered room 252 first. I had my phone in my hand and I put 252 in the body of a text. But I didn't know who to send it to so I closed the phone again and followed him in. He hadn't turned the lights on. I heard him open the drawer where the Bible was and put something heavy, metallic in there. The door closed behind me and I leaned back against it just as he bent over the table where the television was and turned on the lamp. The white walls were rimmed in Pepto Bismal. He straightened, careful not to look at himself in the mirror. His large military duffel propped against the wall under the window to the left of the door, the ashtray clean and the bed made like it hadn't been slept in.

Then it felt ridiculous and cheap to fuck a stranger in a motel. Typical drunk girl move. Fuck a hobo, something to make the party people talk. Which might be better than to be forgotten. Maybe. But a different kind of girl wouldn't think of leaving a bar with some guy like this. A different kind of girl wouldn't have ditched Lydia and Audrey and Bridget to drink at Charlie's with a stranger. But I had. Because I wasn't somebody else, I was nothing in the first place, which is what started this whole mess.

Maybe he *did* think something of me. But that was stupid. So maybe he only wished I'd leave. Just get out of his fucking room. It was possible he'd been making it obvious the whole time, and I hadn't got it, kept hanging around. It was possible I'd imagined the whole thing, made it out of thin air and what I'd seen on television. Or maybe he was just using me to get to the untouchable one. Or he was one of those weirdo fucks who'd tie me to the bed and cut off the soles of my feet.

You know, I said. I think maybe I had too much to drink. I think I'd better. Go. You don't have to.

He was holding the pack in his arms, looking around like he wanted a place to hide it. He didn't say anything. He didn't want me here. Or if he did it would be the evening news. Missing. Dead. It was stupid to leave but I couldn't stay.

Yeah, I said. I think I'll just, go.

I turned weirdly on my heel and opened the door. I didn't look behind me and stepped back into the pink smoke outside. The door shut again and I walked fast skimming my hand on the cool balcony railing. I hummed embarrassedly to myself, stumbling loudly down the stairs. Fool, I thought. Across the street the bank clock flashed 3:36 a.m. Even the cops were off duty. I turned slowly when he said my name.

Damn you didn't give me a chance to ask you to stay.

I turned to see James standing at the foot of the stairs, at the edge of the parking lot. He walked toward me and stopped a little ways off to roll a cigarette. He lit it, took a hard pull, and handed it to me through its own smoke. He rolled another one and lit that. We stood in the lot near the sidewalk where the cement parking space dividers were.

I'm not going to hurt you, he said. If that's what you're thinking.

I thought maybe, I said. I was imagining things. Don't want to be *that* kind of girl.

What kind? he said.

I shrugged. You know, I said. Desperate.

I guess I'm looking for something, he said. He looked at the wound on his palm. I'm asking you, he said. Just stay. I think it'd be better. Not to fight. He dropped his cigarette and stubbed it out with the toe of his boot.

Fight? I said.

He laughed and flicked his busted lip with the back of his little finger. Not for the drama of it, but like an instinct. I watched him from under my eyes and I smiled, at the difference between a touch and a strike, at the difference between that fighting and this.

I figure, he said. All things happen for a reason. Come back around. Full circle.

I wasn't sure I knew what he meant but I felt a kind of understanding in me. We stood silent under the pink lights in the parking lot until he reached across and dragged his finger lightly down my cheek. He rubbed his hair and paced the circle of his cage.

I'm sorry, he said. I'm just. Talking nonsense. You should go. If you want.

I tried to think of something to say. I could go get us a couple Cokes, I said. Or something.

He stepped toward me. How about a kiss?

Then I was following him back up the stairs and I didn't care what happened. Inside the room again I looked around like it was *really* something but it was ugly. The walls slick with fresh white paint and the framed print of ducks in flight looked nailed to the wall. I put my hands in my pockets. He turned, rubbing his mouth worriedly. But when he glanced up he shoved me up against the door. I had his lip in my mouth. I had my eyes open until he did. With me leaning forward and him back we fell against the mattress draped with the plasticene coverlet and in our mouth there was a metallic flavor, the taste of blood.

TWENTY-EIGHT

We weren't asleep when the sky blushed. In the new light the motel room's sanitized white swallowed us. Like a cell, like a trap. To the east the sun still hid behind the foothills that walled in the valley. But we wouldn't see the sun when it rose, it would keep behind the hedge of smoke. Where they met, the same little hills turned violent and erupted in stone faces and shards that cascaded down whole slopes, chasing the river for miles out of sight.

I crept from bed naked and opened the salmon vinyl curtain partly so I could look out the picture window at the faint cool morning. I watched his eyelids, which were closed, crept to the bed and lay back down. Out the window, the riverbank and the backlit hills. Above the top of the canyon, the smoke. I was careful not to move.

You asleep? he said.

Not in the least.

He looked right at me, his wild eyes wide. Maybe he was afraid. Maybe I was. I didn't sleep at all, he said.

He wrenched himself from bed. I sat smoking with the polyester sheet draped over my breasts. In the mirror his reflection swayed and looked out the reflection of the picture window at Broadway, then at the thick gray sky, which wasn't visible in the mirror. The pink parking lot lights were off during day but in the room their presence remained. The bedspread was teal with evenly spaced red spots. Beneath it in the mirror I looked stained an olive green, with a purple bruise near one knee. But what's visible is easily mistaken, at a distance. I rearranged myself at an angle and pursed my lips, checked to see if James was watching, but he still watched the sky.

We should go out, he said. Shouldn't just stay here. Waiting.

It was morning so I could see there was some kind of change between us even though it'd only been one night. A kind of resignation, at least for now. It was more than other people will ever have had. He glanced at his cut palm.

Outside, he said slowly. I don't know why this thing won't heal up.

The old smoke stink hung sour in the plastic and the polyester. He got up, got a little stack of bent photos from the side of the pack, and stood looking at them with his back to me before he put them back. I watched him, pulled my wrist to me and the cigarette followed. When he turned around he glared out the window like he saw someone he recognized rifling through the dumpster, turned his eyes on me, one framed in piss yellow and black. I could see the wind was up again, stoking the blazes, dragging the smoke down to my level.

What? I said. What is it?

He sat at the foot of the bed with his back to me rubbing his face as if he could rub the last of his drunk off.

You better ash that, he said.

The tiny ash cylinder between my fingers curled at the tip, ready to collapse. So much time had passed, I hadn't realized.

There's, he said. Somebody watching me. They know I'm here.

I laughed. What, like in Montana?

In Montana, he said. In Missoula, at this motel probably maybe watching us in this room right now.

He hadn't turned. I squinted to try and see his eyes in the mirror. So he was crazy, paranoid. Unless.

Somebody's, I said. Following you?

And he wants me dead, he said. Just like.

I reached out to touch his naked shoulder with my fingertips but he moved away and shook his head and stood.

That's it, that's it, he said. Do it all over again. Like I'm my pops, not dead yet.

I didn't say anything. When he glanced at me his face dropped.

Forget it, he said. You wouldn't believe it if I told you. You're already wondering. So what, is he nuts? You've been wondering that since the beginning.

He turned to look at me over his shoulder and his burning red eyes looking for confirmation. I didn't know what to say. It wasn't as if he'd confessed some elaborate delusion. I didn't have much to go on, I didn't know him, I didn't know what to think. With my eyes I tried to say I believed him, anything, whatever it was. But when I thought on it logically, he was a stranger.

He could be crazy. He nodded once and stood up. Like he'd heard what I'd said in my head.

Smells like shit in here, he said.

He opened the door and the room filled with invisible smoke. He turned in the doorway, his silhouette walking toward me blocked the gray light. He stood over me. His hand slipped down my cheek and curled around my chin and he tilted my face back and leaned down to kiss me as if he would keep doing it softly.

TWENTY-NINE

James had his jeans on again and sat at the edge of the bed with his wrists draped between his knees. He opened the drawer where the Bible was like he was checking to make sure it was still there. Tattoo behind his ear. His face less swollen, a bruise spreading across his temple, not a black eye exactly. It scared me and I reached out like a reflex. But when I brushed his back lightly with the tips of my fingers, he flinched.

Sorry, he said and touched his lip.

Been kind of jumpy. Since the fight, he said. At the camp by the river. Fucker's name's Bong, if you can believe it. Had some kind of mouth on him. Started trash talking at me, which is something I do not tolerate.

His arms were dark from the sun but his sides and stomach were pale, and there was a large, light bruise seeping up his ribcage from the front.

Can't talk to an asshole like that, he said. Can't reason with them. Only thing they understand is this.

He grabbed my wrist, too hard. He sighed and looked away.

You want to get out of here? he said.

My wrist still stung.

Where to?

You tell me, he said.

Sit by the river? I said and glanced at him.

He didn't say anything, like he was deciding.

Sure, he said. I'll pick the spot. You can read. He pointed at *The Waves* falling from my bag on the floor next to the bed. If you want, he shrugged.

In the bathroom I scrubbed my face in the measly drizzle of cold water. There wasn't a window. There was never a window or the window didn't open. My hands shook and my hung-over reflection with all that flat black hair. I slicked on my lipstick in the bad light and got my face organized before I opened the door. James stood in the doorway blowing smoke at the smoke with his shirt in his hand.

Bright out, I said.

I wondered if whomever was supposed to be following him was out there now, if they were watching each other, or if James thought so. Someone was always watching. My big purse dirty on the floor. My phone was in there. I rifled around and found it, flipped it open so he wouldn't see, wouldn't think I was one of those girls, addicted to her phone. There was a missed call from Bridget but no message.

I'd hold your hand, he said in the parking lot.

I shrugged. In the doorway the smoke had stopped my breath. And then I only breathed in sips. My eyes watered, burned, my lips cracking, my throat and mind so parched in this desiccated haze. I didn't mention it. I knew it made no difference if I said anything. If I ever said anything again or if he did. Because it was all customary, playing things out for embarrassment, pretending to believe in a world you could describe. Pretending to believe in an out there, in an in here. Maybe he understood we were lying when we opened our mouths to blah blah blah, that the truth was something else.

He walked just ahead of me. His black Levis sagged in the ass like something was dragging them down from inside. My lungs full of smoke and invisible ash fell, but I'd pick white flecks from my hair and shoulders. It meant something, how the ash did not appear in the air but then did appear on the body. Hair, backs of the hands, tops of the shoes. Hellgate Canyon impossible behind the filthy smoke. I knew it was there, but it was invisible. Although if I approached, it would overcome me, larger than life. This seemed important. A wind started, strongish, and it blew a bit of trash up the street, a plastic bag and a wrapper. But this was no *American Beauty.*

THIRTY

At the Government Liquor Store downtown I paid for the booze with a wrinkled ten-dollar bill I'd found in the laundry. By three o'clock we were drinking vodka lemonades by the river. Despite the smoke it was hot. Despite the smoke we were outside, tucked against the power plant's substation with high fences and barbed wire that enclosed rows of transformers big as train cars with taut electrical wires and artificial tumors protruding on all sides. Every breath was a nightmare. The air was concrete walls closing in on us all the time, isolating us here in this puny spot like a cell with only the fence, the barbed wire, and the skeleton of the bridge visible.

Soon it was almost rush hour. It smelled like burning, burning, and the visible people became indistinct, shrinking into the distance and the smoke. I had *The Waves* open but I couldn't read. My dry mind, the smoke. It muddled me, or the booze did, or it was nothing in particular. There was no excuse for how I'd become. James read aloud sometimes but otherwise we didn't talk. He was reading a play called *The Pillowman.*

I *tried* to listen, something about an interrogation, but the words frightened me, so instead I watched the river. I'd be out of money soon. I had maybe a hundred bucks left. And sometimes George's checks came after rent was due. Which meant I needed a plan, an out. From my apartment, from this town, this valley. From this life. For now I was just like anybody, taking refuge in the river. But upstream was a Superfund site; everything downstream was probably poisoned. Still people's pink bodies hovered just above the water atop fat rubber inner tubes or hidden legs. And James read. He read well, slowly and with little emotion. I wasn't listening until he said, Where is my brother, what have you done to my brother. He stopped and looked up, but not at me.

The sun a hazy, dusty mass.

Once I was drunk, I fell asleep and flicked the spiders off without opening my eyes until I woke with a dry mouth and a swarm of ants on the place in the grass where my drink had spilled. I knew I was uglier than usual, the yellow dress, and James sat farther off with his hands clasped over his knees watching me. I sat up. Our eyes were brown. He was dressed perfectly; his clothing fit him as a bird's feathers fit its body. In the distance dwarfed adults trundled across the bridge, pushing strollers. A cruiser with its red lights flashing, everybody on the bridge turned to stare.

Soon we lay side by side in the dry grass.

I would've kissed him; I liked his smell now. His breath wasn't citric or sweet like vodka lemonade, only musty with cigarettes. He sat up to roll and light one. I'd have asked, but he already offered like we were used to this. The cigarette smooth and delicate.

At dusk the dry haze and smoke remained, so we moved closer to the water slipping past thick-black as oil. By dark we sat on a tiny scrap of sandy beach, waiting for something to happen. After a little while bats started to flit on the shell of the water as if they'd burst from underneath.

The bats, I said. They're coming out of the river!

James didn't say anything and watched. Their slim black masses rising like dawn at an angle, like gunshots, and they'd fall again and rise, and rise. I'd always been disgusted by bats, like rats tight in skin-sacks with an insect's overgrown wings and would've worried one might be caught in my hair. But I'd read about them, and now I admired them, how they inhabited abandoned buildings, filled empty houses and churches with black life, and the night.

THIRTY-ONE

We hadn't talked about my apartment yet, not since I first mentioned it. I could've offered, but instead I followed him without speaking, back to the Bel Aire. The room stank. It was the cheap carpet, the years of stale smoke, the filthy gasses coming off the polyester coverlet. My reflection moved on the window black with the night. Maybe someone was watching. I pulled the blind shut. He crouched down then, glanced back at me pretending not to watch him. He took something he had tucked into the back of his pants, wrapped it in a shirt, and put it all at the top of his pack. The way he held his body to try and hide whatever-it-was from view, but I'd seen its dull glisten.

What is that? I said without thinking.

I sat cross-legged and my body divided into perfect halves. Behind him we were reflected hypnotically in the mirror. Even our dark hair matched, our thinness. My eyes sunken with the liquor and we hadn't eaten anything although it was after eleven.

It's a gun. He didn't smile. Do you believe me?

I shrugged.

That's good, he said.

He touched my head, my hair, in a rough way as if he'd suddenly become unaccustomed to touching a girl. My head dropped with his hand. He took several steps backward watching me and I shifted slightly to take a more enticing pose but the broken springs made a big sound.

Impatient? he said, coming toward me.

We fell asleep sweating, our skin stuck together. He had one arm beneath my neck, and held me to him with the other. When I whispered his name he only clutched me tighter. I needed to use the bathroom but couldn't move. I looked closely at his lids—lightly red like a polluted sunrise—and the thick black lashes. There was something childish in it, like how a scared kid grips its mommy in disaster. Genocide, air raid, end times. I imagined him alone, sitting on the highway shoulder, on the gravel and I softly kissed his slack mouth. It was good to be held even if I couldn't move. I wanted to cry, but I knew I wouldn't. There were water spots on the ceiling. The air conditioning unit trilled but wasn't doing much. We could've opened a window, but they were bolted shut.

His arm loose across me in the morning when I woke thirsty, parched, and facing the window. Beyond it clouds lolled around the South Hills all spackled with ranch homes. Any other day I would've woke up thinking, Bridget, Bridget. I rolled to look at him. The bed rocked and he woke or pretended to. He opened his eyes and his busted lip cracked, but he didn't seem to notice. His cut hand came up between us but he paused before he touched me.

It feels good, he said. To be here with you. Like I could stay with you a while.

It was just a line. But I didn't know what he really wanted. Still, if he was my boyfriend, Bridget wouldn't matter anymore.

She could ditch me if she wanted to. He petted my forehead awkwardly with his fingers.

Thanks? I said. And smiled thinly, my head on my arm. I hoped I looked all right, staring back at him. But I was uncomfortable naked, now that it was daylight. I should've gotten up and checked my face, made up myself when he was still asleep.

Want some water? he said.

He brought himself upright with an effort, swung his legs over the side of the bed and sat with his back to me. His vertebrae and ribs patterned his back intricate as a strip of lace. Sallow bruises spread up from his spleen. I should've gotten up too, to fix myself up, but that would've made his offer pointless. So I posed and pretended to fall asleep. When he sat again the cheap mattress bowed and I pretended to wake again. He held a little plastic cup of water. I took it with both hands, drank. It tasted like bad pipes and plastic.

Good? he said.

I nodded, and shook the upside down cup at my mouth like more might appear, watched one drop move sluggishly across the bottom.

More? he said.

Oh I can get it, I said.

I moved like to get up but he brought up another little plastic cup from the floor. I smiled at the water and took it and drank.

More?

It was just tap water, but I laughed like it was such a gift and left my hands with the empty cups on the polyester sheet. He brought up another from the floor and I drank that. Long fingers, thin toes, he was better than I could've hoped for. I smiled for real, maybe for the first time, and he pretended to, so soon we were grinning stupidly like kids. In a sweep he brushed the cups to the floor where they fell with a muffled tinkle. He leaned to me like he'd kiss me but didn't, our foreheads touched and he leaned back again. I stared down at the ugly carpet, stained with brown bruises. It was a horrible room. He must've heard me think it.

Maybe I could crash, he said. At your place? I mean. I got to get out of this room.

I glanced up at him but he kept his eyes on the floor. It wasn't a question. There wasn't a real choice; the only answer was yes. I swallowed.

At my place?

Was I afraid? He wasn't a hobo really. Maybe he'd give me money if I let him stay. But he wanted something else from me: my life, I didn't know. I didn't want to let him but I knew I would. He didn't look up. I had to say yes. When I laughed he looked up at last, and shrugged.

I guess, I said. You can. Like, crash. For a while, if you want.

He nodded. If you're sure, he said.

I'm sure.

No pressure, he said, grinning. Or whatever.

Which was a lie.

I mean, it's not like you're moving in, I said. But my place, it's like, a couple blocks from here. It's stupid to. Pay for a motel when.

Sure. Your call. He held up his hands as if he'd surrender.

It's dumb, I said. You with a motel.

You said that, he said and smiled.

THIRTY-TWO

I'm sorry it's a mess.

I must've left the door unlocked. I checked the mail but George's check hadn't come. So I put some minimal music on, echoes in an abandoned dance hall. Or party house. Behind police barricade. Do Not Cross. I wished it was night, the daylight made everything dull and realistic. I turned on some lights anyway. I had a lot of lamps, mostly from Goodwill. Like one hung from a chain that buzzed intolerably. It was a metal cage with the light bulb and a naked woman inside, her torso arced, she dipped her fingers into water that wasn't there.

James in the foyer like a kid gazing up at the picture postcards I had taped above the door. Those were the flying pictures: some birds, a naked skydiver, and bats. In the kitchen I tried to squash the trash with my hand, to make room for more. Now he stood in the living room with his pack still on, fingering the spines of my books.

In my bedroom I tried to shove the dirty laundry pile inside so I could shut the closet door and was reflected in the cheap mirror tacked inside. I looked desperate. If I had a job still I could've gone shopping already. That's what girls were supposed to do when they got a man. So George's check hadn't come. But it would arrive, anytime. I couldn't remember when; I couldn't remember what day it was. I'd washed my sheets, some time. I shook them out and dropped a couple books on top. I took off my yellow dress and opened the closet door so all the clothes dumped out again.

I yanked another dress, a red cotton one, from the hanger and put it on. In the mirror it looked better than what I'd been wearing for days, but maybe he'd think it was corny if I changed. Desperate. I pulled it off and put the yellow one back on. Limp. Filthy. Ugly. Strange.

Goddamnit, I said.

I pulled it off again and put the red one on. I tugged at my hair, which was flat and too soft from the motel shampoo. But the dress was good, like sunset during the fires. In the living room James sat on the couch reading a book with his pack under his knees. I sat down next to him and he didn't look up.

You want a drink?

He glanced up. You changed. The book closed over his fingers. His other hand palm up, the scab damp and red. He frowned at me for a long time, like he might be disappointed, or thinking about something else. He'd turned the lamps off. The light was thin, the shadows shallow.

What? I said and laughed. You want a drink or not?

What is this supposed to be? he said. You put that dress on for me or what?

I mean, I said. I just. Was wearing that other dress for like three days is all.

Yeah, he said. So you're saying. So you're telling me you just like *happened* to put a *red* dress on. No reason.

His cut hand clenching and unclenching, the other one still as some dead thing, like it was part of the book.

Should I change again? I tried to come up with something to say. I. I. I.

But he'd started talking.

My photos, he was saying. *Somebody* stole them. There was a *wedding* photo. She's wearing a red dress. They gave them back but. You didn't. You didn't.

Then I laughed. What? I said. Steal them?

Nah, he said.

My stomach dropping and him staring blankly at me, like I was a ghost. I don't know what you're talking about, I said. I didn't. I didn't *steal* your pictures. I don't. Even know what you're talking about. I just. Wanted to change my dress. No reason.

Sure, he said. Sure. Sure. I know of course. I didn't really think you.

He ran his fingers through his hair. It was funny I hadn't noticed how oily it was, like he couldn't remember the last time he'd showered. He rubbed his skull.

Sure, he said. I'd love one.

I poured the drinks with my hand shaking, like some fifties housewife, vodkas with club soda and a plastic smile. A valium smile. The valium bottle I kept above the kitchen sink. He'd moved to the floor and sat cross-legged with Robert Frank's *The Americans* open. Photos of Butte in the sixties. Rough-looking miners just before a bar fight. A mess of filthy kids, their big mamma and worn-out daddy behind the wheel. With the mines shut down people don't have to work like that anymore. We shop instead. I put the drinks on the floor. The next picture was of white people, black people, looking startled at the camera out the windows of a bus. He had a stack of snapshots in his hand. But he wasn't looking at those yet.

Reminds me of the beginning of this old Fellini movie, he said. The man's dreaming he's asphyxiating in traffic. All the cars are old, and everybody, all the other drivers, they're just watching him suffocate. He's like beating on the windows and he can't breathe but nobody moves. There's all these people on this bus watching but you can't see their heads, just their arms hanging out the windows like zombies. Then the guy dies in his dream. Floats up. Up. There's the sky.

He drank and turned to look at the snapshots in his hand. The one on top of a man, and a woman in a red dress. His tongue's tip between his teeth. Long teeth, straight and white for how much he smoked. Expensive teeth. And his wide lips bulged like globules of oil. His face unblemished, the new beard coming in coarse and even and black. He liked my stare, I could tell it by his slow smile.

He bent closer to the photo, posing for me. Then handed it to me, looking at his drink. He took a sip. The photo was aging, turning brownish. A woman in a long red dress and a man in cowboy boots and a leather vest, his wide tie loose and his collar unbuttoned. Must've been the seventies. They stood outside, hillside rising up behind them, tall grasses stopped forever in the camera's eye, in my eye. They weren't smiling.

I've never seen it before, I said. Sorry.

The man in the photo looked familiar. But I wouldn't mention it. I couldn't think of where I'd seen him. From around, like everybody else. One vertebrae stretched James's neck skin taut. He looked up.

It's just, he said. Somebody *killed* my father. But I didn't even *know* about him. So like, my whole fucking *life* was just completely rocked before I even got to Montana. And I've been on the road for weeks. Sleeping outside, dealing with all manner of crazy fucking hobos talking all manner of shit. For example I might have a sibling? Not to mention my face is now busted. And I just have this *feeling* things aren't right. Like obviously. And like how my photos just disappeared. And then reappeared. So maybe you can understand. Why I might be a little. Tense. So you come out in a red dress. I guess I'm just. On edge.

He was out of breath. Maybe it was the smoke.

All right, I said. So there's no problem. So like, my *outfit* has nothing to do with it.

Ever since I got here, he said. It's all repeating almost. I mean, I don't even know for sure he was murdered. But everybody I meet, it's like they're in on it. Everybody's trying to fuck with me.

He was looking at the floor talking, confiding in me. I was trying to listen, to understand. Like a girlfriend. My cellphone on the coffee table vibrated toward the edge, a wind-up toy. I snatched at it. It was Bridget. I'd forgotten about Bridget. I didn't answer.

I think you're just paranoid, I said. I mean, you just found out? If it's been thirty years he must've been dead before you were born. What did you think happened, all that time before?

I didn't know, he said. I didn't *know*.

I waited. He'd changed his mind about me. Accusing me meant he could repent, he could confess as if it was the same as an apology. So he'd decided he could use me, he was weakening and he'd tell me the truth now. If I didn't interrupt and break the spell. Even if it was some big hallucination I'd have something on him, collateral. Something to use against him and make him stay. I finished my drink.

And now I run into this old guy, he said. And his woman, she says something like my dad had another kid or something? He was just some. Crazy old fucker. Thought he saw a ghost, me standing there looking like my pops. His woman was probably nuts too. I shouldn't let it get to me. I should just forget it.

He rubbed his skull. He ran his fingers through his slick hair. I held the phone in both hands to see if Bridget would leave a message. He was telling me something important. I wouldn't let Bridget ruin it. I would answer next time. Next time.

Wait, I said. A long-lost sibling? That's awesome. It's like something from a movie.

Which, it seemed, was what he wanted to hear. He grinned. I tried a little more.

You're like, I said. A detective. Like Philip Marlowe.

Yeah right, he said. All I need now is some Scotch.

Scotch I've got, I said and stood up.

The vodka was working. The valium was working.

So what, I said. You're going to like, look for clues?

It was a joke but I waved my hand at his photographs. He shrugged. I wanted the Scotch. I needed the Scotch. But not as much as before. I didn't think about Bridget. I focused on the Evil Eye tattooed behind his ear.

I don't really know what I'm looking for, he said. I'm still like sorting it all out. You know, I didn't even know he was my father until a month ago. So that's a trip.

That's putting it mildly, I said. Which was a cliché. I took his glass and was already on my way out of the room. What's his name? I hollered. Your dad, I mean.

The filthy kitchen made me realize how hungry I was. I was starving. I was ravenous. I took a pull from the bottle before I poured his glass, then mine. I opened the fridge but there wasn't anything really. He must've been mumbling, or I wasn't listening because I couldn't hear the name.

THIRTY-THREE

He'd been staying at my place for three days when the Fish Creek fire started. Of course it seemed worse than it was since Fish Creek is west and the weather always comes from that direction, over the Bitterroots. What happened was some Pacific storm rolled inland through Seattle with winds up to fifty miles an hour. Just blasted the Eastern Washington fires so they raged into Idaho, to Montana eating up grasslands and larch and pondy pines for miles. So the winds from the west grew, smoke pouring into the valley, thicker than you can imagine.

George's check still hadn't come. James hadn't given me any money and I hadn't asked even though I didn't have any food at my place. Or hardly any booze, eventually. I only had like twenty bucks left. I didn't know what to do. We'd been stuck in there for days already. Talking, not talking, fucking, drinking. I don't know what all. James talked mostly. About his stepdaddy Dick, about the daddy he never knew. Mostly he was making shit up. He even told me so. And I'd tell you what else he said if I could remember, but I can't. Because I was drinking, drunk, I wasn't listening. Because he never wanted to leave, never wanted to go outside, and it wasn't just the smoke.

Maybe we had the bends.

It took everything to get him down to Charlie's for a drink. Gus, Irene, and Blaise were there like always. Charlie let them live for free in the apartments below mine. Sounds like charity, but it's business. Keep your drunks on the premises. James paid for our bottles of Pabst. We got one of the tall tables behind the pool table.

My phone vibrated in my pocket. Bridget.

I had to answer. This time I had to.

She'd called so many times. But I'd hesitated too long and the screen said Missed. Which was only a temporary relief; she was calling again.

It's uh Bridget? My friend? I said. From the party. She keeps calling. I better.

I started toward the door.

Hello?

Ruth? she said. Fuck where *are* you? I've called you like a million times. Because. Well I can't believe you just ditched me the other night. I mean, I was having a really bad week. And you never called *me*. That's so. I don't know, I don't know, Ruth, that's just not. You know what I'm saying? I mean. Where *are* you?

I could've just called her. It would've been easier if I'd just called. And now it was a *thing*. Her voice droning in my ear, my mind raw. If I'd wanted to be a good friend, I would've called after I'd seen what she did to her place; I wouldn't have left her at the Badlander in the first place. But I hadn't even thought about that because I didn't really care. I pushed the door open. Bits of ash fell and an unnatural wind had started. It whipped up the trash in the street.

Uh Charlie's?

You're *always* at Charlie's, she said. I thought you were *dead*.

So I was guilty. I knew, I understood. But I wouldn't admit it, which would only make things worse. The hot phone, her voice burning into my skull.

Is that where you disappeared? she said. I haven't seen you in a *week*. In *two* weeks, except that night. Before you. *Bounced*.

I *texted* you, I said.

What?

I said I *texted* you. When I left. We're not like. *Married*.

I'd never said anything like that to Bridget before. There'd never *been* anything but her before. I didn't need her if I had a boyfriend. But he *wasn't* my boyfriend.

Is this like a fuck you? she said. Is this like your new thing? I paid for your *dinner*, Ruth, you know what I'm saying? I told Lydia and Audrey you were there and they were really. Excited. And then you were just *gone*. That was totally. I mean I called you and you didn't answer, you know what I'm saying?

It seemed unlikely that Lydia and Audrey had been excited to hang out with me.

Look I, I said. I.

But I had nothing.

Okay well whatever, she said. Just like let's forget it. I'm almost there anyway.

Here?

I was pacing, watching my reflection in the window of the pawnshop next door. The display guns aimed through my translucent forehead. I tried to picture Bridget and James making conversation. It didn't come out well.

I can see you, Ruth, she taunted. Can you see me?

Her truck paused at the red light on the corner, blinker flashing.

Well I'm here with, I said. I just met this. I pictured the Evil Eye.

What? she said. A *guy*?

I should've thought of this. Boyfriend potential was the only thing Bridget would accept for why I'd left without saying goodbye. It'd been something that bothered her about me since the beginning. That I never had a man. Partly it was because they always went for Bridget. Always. Even James had. And if they met again, I couldn't say.

He was mine. Mine.

Yeah, I said, watching the truck's blinker. A guy.

Well, I won't *bother* you, she said. I'll just drink my drink, and then I'll go.

It was stupid to be talking on the phone. She was right there in her truck, she was keeping me from going inside to prepare James. And then she'd come in all lit on fire like a Roman candle. Even without trying, she always knew how to work a room. God I wanted to go in and warn him. Turn him against her. Enough, but not too much. Before she either told him to his face he was a piece of shit or acted super *into* whatever *he* was into. Which in this case was his daddy.

She had the windows up against the smoke, the AC on.

Or whatever, she said. I should probably tell you if he's a total freak.

Look, I said. I'm hanging up okay? I'll see you in there.

That was rude.

Oh my God, Bridget. I'll see you in *two* seconds.

Just *wait* a second, she said.

She'd gotten out of the truck and was looking for a break in traffic. A cruiser with two cops inside stopped for her and she started to cross, looking gorgeous like always in sandals, black shorts and a nearly transparent pin-striped tank. The cops watched her, not smiling but they liked the show. She looked better than the last time I saw her. Her dark, slant eyes and brows, her Monroe hair, like a disguise. I hung up.

She didn't flip her phone shut until she was standing in front of me.

I thought you'd like apologize, she said. I thought you'd be sorry.

I did not want this. If she was pissed, she might be a bitch to me in front of James, or she might be a bitch to James, although that was rare when it came to men.

Look, I'm sorry, I said. I'm sorry.

You don't *have* to apologize, she said.

Which was bullshit on her part, a line. But maybe I meant what I was saying.

I, I said. I *am* sorry. I was trying to feel it, inside. I wasn't sure if it was working.

No it's cool, Ruth, she said. You don't have to apologize.

She smiled a little but I imagined there was something else in the look like jealousy. That was good. I hoped she'd be hurt by me finding someone besides her, even though that was supposed to be the point of girlfriends, to get a man.

Well, I said. I figured you've been hanging out with Audrey and Lydia.

It's not like we're *together*, she said.

She snorted, like I was the joke.

So are you going to introduce me to your *boyfriend*? she said. Or is it like, a secret. He's in there, isn't he in Charlie's? She cocked her chin at the door.

Inside they didn't shake hands but the way they met wasn't awkward. It's just people don't shake hands anymore, people don't stand up for ladies or touch at all or look you in the eye if possible. They just kind of said hey and glanced at each other although maybe they looked a little longer than that. Then Bridget checked her phone and James looked up at the televisions like he'd been watching something interesting all the time. And he took a sip of his beer and things were all right.

Ruth probably hasn't mentioned me at all, she laughed.

I've heard about you.

I hadn't mentioned her, I hadn't told him anything. I thought she probably hadn't mentioned me at all, she said again. She didn't look at me.

I *met* you, he said. You don't remember?

She glanced up and scanned his face and frowned.

They actually have a pretty good steak here, she said. Whenever my mom got all drunk and lonely, we'd end up here for steaks. Typical. But I haven't had one in forever.

She looked good and she glanced up at James. He'd been watching her hard with some kind of stare. She stood up to order. The drinks dulled the hole in my stomach. I'd want another drink; I didn't have enough money to eat. I could tell he was trying not to watch her walk away. I tried to come up with something to say. Something like, What, you want her? But didn't. James watched the televisions. His Evil Eye watched me.

You met, I said. At the party, I think.

I know where I met her.

Like he wished I'd shut up. I drank. Bridget with a Bloody Mary. She stared frankly at James who shifted in his seat and ahemed, his eyes on the television like he could feel her watching him and he liked it. I looked back at Bridget, who drank from the straw so that she might hide her smile. She looked up but not at me exactly.

When you disappeared, she said. I just didn't know *what* to think. I'm just glad you're *safe*, Ruth. I was *worried*.

James pretended not to pay attention. I drank. I could've gone to the bathroom, made sure I looked all right. But that meant leaving them alone together. To say whatever it was they weren't saying now. Bridget took nips from the straw, pretending to watch the televisions, her eyes on James who stood up. I looked around at the drunks for something to do. It was nothing but smoke outside and we were all camped out in the dark in here, like refugees. I didn't have any friends besides Bridget and if he took her, or she took him, there'd be no one. He walked to the bar and stood waiting for the bartender.

Who *is* that? Bridget said. He looks like somebody. I mean he looks *exactly* like.

He was *at* the party, I said.

No not like that, she said. Like—

She stopped herself, shook her head.

The cook stood at the table. Bloody, he said and half-dropped the steak plate.

Some watery blood seeped from in it, pooled glistening. She raised her eyebrows once. James was back, put three drinks on the table, two beers and a bloody. Maybe I should've been drinking a bloody, maybe that's what a girl should be drinking, and this beer would make me fat although cool girls drank beer sometimes, I thought.

Thanks, I said.

You drink this, Ruth, Bridget said. I'd never be able to drink *two* bloodies.

Which was a lie. She was half-through the first one already and hadn't even started on the steak. She'd just said it to sound pretty, she'd just said it for James.

Ruth can drink anything, she told James. She could drink you under the table.

God I hated her. I hated her.

Extra plate, the cook said.

I'll bet you can manage, James told her and cleared his throat.

It was weirdly gentlemanly, the way he said it. He didn't look at anybody. Bridget unwrapped the paper napkin from around the bent fork and knife and slipped the fries and salad onto the extra plate. The steak alone, its watery blood pooled where the sides had been. James picked up a fry.

You going to eat these? he said.

Bridget shrugged. He put it back down.

It's sick, you know, the pig lard they use for their fryer and the pigs anymore they're so fat they're blind.

James laughed like that was just about the wittiest thing he'd heard. Beef much different then?

I could never give it up, she said.

She had a piece of the meat skewered and she removed it from the fork with her teeth. Her lipstick dull, not glossed like normal. It was a good look for her, the color dark but redder than the meat, making her teeth white as a vampire's.

She'd seen the cut on his hand. And he glanced down too,

then up again at that mouth, at those dark lips as if he'd like to fuck them. Bridget all chick lust and pride with her eyes glinting like gasoline vapor on the air. Forever passed. I drank and looked away.

What happened to your hand? she cooed.

Cut it, he said.

She laughed.

I can *see* that, she said.

There was a pause.

You had quite the effect on Ruth, she said. Usually she calls like every day.

Which was a lie, I thought. I thought it was a lie.

I knew it must've been someone, she said but didn't finish.

I was slouching toward the table now. James looked over but didn't touch me. If he cared he could've touched me. Bridget had finished her first bloody but hadn't touched the second. I was so hungry. I was starving, a raw gnaw in my gut. And there was this plate of fries, right there in front of me. But *they* weren't touching them, *they* weren't looking at them even, and if they didn't I couldn't like I was a pig.

You can *have* the fries, Ruth. Bridget laughed. God you're like, boring a hole in them you're staring so hard.

Oh I. I just, I said. I was just. Staring into space is all.

James pushed the plate toward me like it was something disgusting or like they were in on it together. Against me. If that was so, I wasn't going to *do* what they wanted me to do. I wasn't going to *eat* anything. I'd be so thin, I'd eat nothing, I'd quit drinking and if I quit drinking. But I couldn't do that.

I'm not hungry, I said. Thanks.

I got out a cigarette.

If you're not going to, James said.

I shrugged like I didn't care. Him with the ketchup, chewing. The smell of hot oil and salt. My mouth wet. I looked away.

Well, James said and swallowed and drank. Well, I am that. Somebody.

Bridget laughed. Oh?

A big nobody, he said. At least in this town. Not like my pops, from what I hear.

This town's full of fucking legends, I said and stood up and swayed. Anyone need a drink?

I shouldn't have been drunk yet. I didn't want to listen to their blah blah anymore. I would not be drunk yet, I was not drunk yet. I turned and walked slowly toward the bar. If I just hung my head down a little I'd be all right, I'd feel all right with my head down a little like that. There was a hand on my back.

You all right? James said.

I stepped back and folded my arms.

Why wouldn't I be? I said. You want a drink?

I got it, he said.

No, I said. I'll get them. Seriously.

I had my money out, a damp wad of crumpled bills. It was the last of my cash, but I didn't care. He put his large palm over the bills and my hands.

Seriously, he said.

But I pulled away and stepped up to the bar. I didn't need anything from him. I'll fucking *get* it, I said and didn't look.

He didn't say anything else. I regretted it but what could I do now? Nothing. He must've gone back to the table because he was sitting again when I brought the drinks over. A beer, a bloody, and a vodka on the rocks. I could carry three at once because I was a fucking professional nobody, because I'd done this waiting for a living. Bridget still hadn't touched the second one, like she was trying to show me up, to fuck with me. She'd gotten a newspaper somehow and she was reading it like she really gave a shit. I'd never seen Bridget read the paper before. She glanced up.

I haven't *touched* this one, she said and laughed to insult me.

Then I'll drink it, I said.

I bent the straw over the side of the fresh bloody glass and drank three thirsty swallows so I could dump the vodka rocks right in. But the glass overflowed, spilled the red sludge on the table. Them just watching me like I was shit but I didn't care.

Shit, I said and wiped it with my hand as best I could.

Before I forget, Bridget said. Here.

She pulled an envelope from her bag, an envelope with my name on it. I didn't know the handwriting. I sat carefully on the tall stool looking at my name. Ruth. Ruth. There was a dead Ruth, and there was me. The envelope didn't specify.

Take it, Bridget said.

The envelope smooth and cool from the conditioned air in her truck.

I'm having a party, she said. It's The Party at the End of the World. Lydia came up with that. Like as a joke, but seriously. Just look around.

This is the end, my only friend, James agreed and smiled. May we all get drunk.

I rubbed my thumb across the Ruth. I didn't have the money for another party. I didn't have *any* money. A party, I said.

It's going to be good, she said. We're going to decorate, but it's a secret. You'll love it. There'll be like some drink I haven't decided what yet. Something that goes with the theme. End Times. You *have* to dress up. It'll be fun. I've been meaning to have people over for forever.

What'd you do about the cops? I said.

I *told* you, Ruth, Bridget said. They can't do anything. Not about *this*.

Like the other party? James said. Your place must be. Big.

This'll be different, she said. More. Intimate.

THIRTY-FOUR

Your friend, James told me. I must know her.

What the fuck is that supposed to mean anyway? I said and sat up.

I lit a cigarette for emphasis. It was the next morning or afternoon. The smoke standardized the light, and made it hard to tell. We were still in bed on the floor. I was sick of hearing him say it. Again and again. I couldn't remember everything from the night, but I was pretty sure there hadn't been any problem besides over the drinks, and things were supposed to be okay between us. There was something strange with Bridget. And him. But nothing had happened yet which meant I had to try and keep him.

Is that like, your way of saying you want to fuck somebody? I said. That's all you ever fucking say. You need some new material. I mean seriously.

But he wasn't listening, wasn't looking at me. As if I wasn't there.

It's like, I've seen her picture, he said. Her eyes, they look like. Has she modeled?

No, I said and laughed cruelly, like the idea was ridiculous. She's never *modeled*.

If we could just stay here, in this room, in this apartment maybe he'd forget Bridget. After all, he'd started off saying *your friend*, like she was expendable, like she was the extra. I hadn't opened the invitation yet. Ruth. I could see it, the envelope smooth and white on the bureau over his shoulder. He curled a tendril of my hair around his pointer finger. Light moved through the dust slats that decorated the air in the room and warmed a large rectangular patch of the floor.

She isn't blond really, you know, I said.

As if it mattered. We lay on our sides facing each other with a down pillow in a silk case, our heads on our forearms. Kids in a fort making up ghost stories.

I don't want to leave this room.

That's obvious, he said.

Ever, I said. Her hair's kind of.

I ran my fingers along the skin on his skull.

Your color, I said.

He stopped, like he'd just remembered something.

But I ignored it, and laughed again but it came out loud and harsh and I sat up embarrassed. If I could've kept them from meeting he might not be falling for her over me already, like everybody.

Bridget.

He said it slowly, like he'd forgotten her name or like he was trying to remember something but couldn't. Then he forgot me too and rolled onto his back. He tilted his head to look out the window above us. I knew what you could see through that window. It was the tops of false fronts and satellite disks, lightning rods and tar. Not the street, only rooftops and the sky. But it wasn't the sky, it was only smoke.

You want to go to her party, he said. Her End Times Party.

It wasn't a matter of wanting to or not, but he wouldn't understand.

Look I, I said. I.

I wanted to say I love you but it was too soon and anyway maybe it would've been a lie. I wanted his attention back, like the last few days. I wouldn't lose him to Bridget now. I couldn't lose him to her; James was mine. Maybe George's check would come today, and I could pay rent and we could stay, just like this. Otherwise. He still looked out the window. He sat up and scanned the room, lifted a hand to smooth my right eyebrow.

If she wants something, he said. She'll get it. She always does, doesn't she?

But he already knew the answer. He sighed.

You mean you, I said. Do you mean she'll get you?

I'd said it harshly, and it set the whole situation on edge. In the long pause we were like enemies watching for a weakness in the other, for a flaw. Or like lovers do. It was funny how fast the feeling had changed between us, from one second to the next. Although it might've been this way from the beginning. Ruined.

You're jealous, he said.

You're an asshole, I said. You know that?

It felt scripted. Hollow. Fake. I didn't really mean it but his voice rose. Maybe we weren't only pretending.

What, you want to make me yours? he said. You want to *own* me? You don't even know what I'm thinking. You have no fucking clue *what* I think of her. You can't imagine what is going through my mind.

He had his hand up near my face. I liked how he might hit me.

But you, he said. I *know* what you're thinking. You're thinking, I won't let her take him. He's mine. Mine.

He snorted. He was right. I wouldn't let Bridget ruin this like she had complete control. I ran the tips of my fingers along the base of his stomach and watched the small dark hairs rise. If we could fuck, he'd forget all this. You could redirect rage like that if you tried, shove it into sex, into the body of another, his into mine like a beating. Tongues and teeth and the cock, your wrists pinned, strands of hair in your mouth. Breathless. Breathless. I wore a heather-green tank that was good for my tits and mushroom colored underpants. But he didn't look. I pushed his hand away.

Bridget is my *friend*, I said. We help each other. I'm not going to *fight* her over anything. Anyway. She wouldn't go for some. Loner. Freak.

I stopped. I shouldn't have said it. He wasn't a freak, that was the whole thing. Maybe I hadn't realized until that moment. The way he was so perfectly put together. Clothes like feathers, the good boots and teeth. He was just a daddy's boy. I didn't know for sure what he'd told me was a lie and what wasn't. Who his daddy was or wasn't, what he was doing here in the first place. But I knew for sure, he was just pretending. His eyes opened like he'd heard what I was thinking. I thought he smiled but then he came at me and I pulled back.

Is that what you think?

On my elbows on the floor, the sheets around my legs. That Bridget wouldn't even *think* about you? Or that you're a. A freak.

He brought his face this close to mine. He was enjoying himself. You don't know shit about me, do you? he said. *Do* you?

He pretended to hit me in the side of the skull with his fist but I could tell we were just pretending. I didn't cry out. I wasn't afraid of him. I was afraid of nothing. The people in town beyond this room always watching, watching. I wasn't afraid of Ruth. Or of this. The game was changing in this room and beyond it. I couldn't understand him but I didn't care. I didn't care since I was already as good as dead or dead.

But you let me in your place anyway, he said. I could be anybody. But you brought me back to your place without even knowing *who* I am.

His eyes burned and I couldn't see his hands. His voice a hiss, spitting in my face. I was standing now, my fist against the side of my head where he'd pretended to hit me. Like an infant, fist to face.

He stood.

It disgusted me how there was no meaning in all this but there was no way to stop it now, there was nowhere else to go. He was up on me breathing down my throat and neck, his breath faintly sour, his face rippling from fake to real and back. I turned away but his breath was deafening. The envelope, the slats of dust, the slats in the floor.

Why? Because you're *lonely*? Because you wish you were *dead*?

Him talking into my eyeballs like I was trash. Like he wished I was too.

Yeah, I said. Yeah I wish I was dead. I'm as good as fucking dead. That's what you want. Isn't it. Isn't it? You just want. Me. Dead.

He laughed once. Yeah. I want you dead.

I couldn't think or breathe. I was gasping like a fish. I had to get out of that room. If I stayed I would suffocate, I would suffocate. His hand tight on my arm.

Look at me, he said. Fucking *look* at me.

I walked toward the door gasping. There was plenty of air. There was smoke in the air, everywhere. His grip that hard like they say like a vice. Whiskey grip on my wrist. I looked, my nostrils flared and fell. This was breathing.

Look around, Ruth, he said. Where is it you'd go?

My lips parted like I'd say something. There was nowhere to go, there was nothing but this. Here, this room now. There was no outside of this at all. His face slurred into a sneer, his teeth bared. This was love? Which meant I was alone. Alone huffing spittle-mist and some angry man with my wrist. There was nowhere but here, no one but him. I fell, I pressed my face to his thin bare chest and wept. It'd been so long. It was very predictable.

I've got you, he said. I've got you, babe, I've got you.

He was stroking my head and hair. He held me by the throat.

After a time I looked up from the slats in the floor and touched his lips. I loved him. My fingers were yellow against his skin and my fingernails long and filthy. I kissed him lightly. His lips parted and so did mine. The tips of our tongues, uncooked flesh and flesh. My face was wet. His hand in my hair so my head went back. His eyes shut.

I closed mine. He was watching me. I didn't want to look at him anymore or kiss him anymore. The light in the room stayed the same. I'd seen something like this before. A mountain road black-dark and twisted. Toward the top I stopped in the shoulder to sit on the hood. The mountains, great beasts there and not there, the fog moving toward me. Then the moon that lit the sky and in a flash night evaporated and it was dawn on the horizons.

THIRTY-FIVE

Soon I stood watching my reflection. I would be sick. He sat on the floor with his ankles crossed, leaning against the wall. I'd put blues music on in the other room. Skip, James said, I'd rather be the devil than be that woman's man. The mirror's glass was filthy, my image hazy.

I could cook him breakfast and watch him eat. Eggs, Bacon, French Toast, Bloodies. Bridget couldn't cook worth a damn, which was why she was always eating out on one credit card or another. I could but didn't, I'd cooked for George all those years. In the mirror my neck was very long, with one pretty bite mark he'd left just above the collar bone.

I looked at his reflection coyly but his eyes were shut, his head tilted back and resting on the wall behind him. I wouldn't disturb him. The kitchen was always dark, with one little window above the sink overflowing with dishes and take-out containers. The floor of lettuce, wine-stained like blood.

I shivered in the doorway in my underwear and tank and good tits again, hating the beige walls and the orange-brown refrigerator. The kitchen like a cell but I had good eggs in that refrigerator. The little bulb in my eyes, I crouched in the light to not vomit.

The door swung shut, the light gone out. In the bathroom I could see his reflection through the open doors in the mirror. He crouched looking through his little stack of dirty photographs again. He had his shirt off. I suppose I knew he had a gun, he'd told me although at the time the truth had been the lie. But now I saw it plainly, stuck in the back of his pants. I turned away, flipped the switch and flooded the bathroom with a sallow light.

I think I have a fever, I said to the toilet.

I spat, watched the pretty ripples. James stood in the doorway. You aren't going to vomit.

I wanted to make you breakfast, I said. I'm sorry.

I'd scrubbed the toilet after the party, before James. But the rest of the bathroom was filthy, dirt matted in the corners on the floor, hair and dust coating the back of the sink and the toilet. Like everything, I thought. A clump of hair in the drain staring back at me, accusing me.

You need to get out of this apartment is all. Get out.

I vomited and James slammed the bathroom door. When I was finished he was in the kitchen making drinks.

THIRTY-SIX

I'd been drunk more or less since I got to Montana. Around here everything looked more natural with a drink in your hand. There was a new fire, in what they called the Rattlesnake, which I guess was a creek or some mountains. That was close, that was part of town, north. There were houses there, and people were getting evacuated by the National Guard or whomever. On television they showed a fat man, spraying a ranch home with flame retardant gel from a flaccid little hose.

The smoke had gotten thick like wet concrete, we couldn't go outside. Which was just as well, all those fuckers after me. I was hiding out, like a refugee. I'd sit in the window watching the street down below. Like I watched Reuben and some buddy straight up passed out, their bloated heads on the concrete. I watched them all morning. I thought maybe they were dead. Hoped they were. People would come by and stare. It was like four hours before Reuben lurched upright. Eventually he staggered out of sight looking around all the time like he could feel me watching him but he couldn't figure out where I was.

It was vodka sodas, it was afternoon, it was little Ruth and me.

The phone rang.

Hi Bridget, Ruth said, faking it.

I was on the couch looking through my photos. Looking at his eyes, my eyes, his, my brows. And I heard her name.

When Ruth hung up she didn't look at me.

Bridget said let's get some dinner, she said. The three of us.

She said it just like that, in two slow sentences all punctuated to show her displeasure. So I shrugged at his dark slant-eyes in the photograph. Something was wrong, like I was breaking the law. But I couldn't say which. I drank, to steel myself. It was just dinner.

Her party's tomorrow, Ruth said. The party.

You want to go? I said.

I'm going, she said. If that's what you mean.

She looked good. Weak and delicate like a half-dead tulip. Her dark hair loose on the sloping pale shoulders, her large eyebrows drawn together and her mouth falling like something was dragging it down from below. Ruth already said yes. Yes to the party, yes to dinner. When it came to Bridget, the answer was always yes.

Bridget even picked the restaurant. With a pink florescent sign, it was all but empty, people were evacuating, not going out to eat. Like the inside of a vodka bottle in there, everything painted blue. The punk waiter and bartender dressed in Dickies like a couple of mechanics and Tom Waits singing about a prostitute in Minneapolis. We sat in a wooden booth by the window so I would've had a view if it wasn't for the smoke. I couldn't see a thing but break lights. And then with sunset the smoke lit up piss-yellow. All through dinner like that behind Bridget's head who must've dressed to match the joint, half punk in black and blue. But she didn't really mean it, she was just trying to get my attention and it was working. I had to be careful not to look too hard, or Ruth might have another little episode, even though I could tell just by looking at her it was probably unavoidable. Still I kept glancing back at the side of Bridget's face, in the break and piss lights, at her slant eyes, at the curved tops of her fingers. I wouldn't say too much to her, I wouldn't ask her any questions, not in front of Ruth. I could wait forever if necessary.

I was trying to figure where I'd seen her. When. Her picture, her face, in real life, before. But I wouldn't ask, I couldn't ask in front of Ruth. Her tank almost translucent, her perfect tits. She was well built. This all just a big fucking joke and I grinned. Ruth saw, but didn't get it so she slumped into the bench beside me, drank her pink wine fast.

It went on like that for a little while. Ruth pushing her food around her plate, drinking. But Bridget ate her steak like what she was which is a pretty girl who's looking to fuck for the fun of it, for the exercise.

My burger rare, bleeding onto the pale bun. Ruth ordered another bottle of wine, the third. It was red this time and we laughed at how it stained our lips and teeth, even Ruth smiled and covered her mouth with her hand. I paid in cash. They didn't try and stop me.

When we left Bridget had her hand on the small of my back, the wildfire wind whipping in from Hellgate Canyon, smoke rolling down from the Rattlesnake. The river moved far beneath us, the trucks that passed packed with furniture, with televisions, the people staring. Maybe they were jealous, me with two girls. Except they probably couldn't see where this was headed. They'd think those two were cousins, or sisters even. But truth be told, it was me and Bridget who looked the most alike.

Up in the Rattlesnake, Bridget said. Everybody's evacuating. But I'm not leaving. Nobody on the North Side will. It's been like this before. Nothing ever happens.

Back at her place, Ruth's lip curled not unlike a snarl just before Bridget kissed her. They were on the couch. There was a certain droop in Ruth always like a willow, even the tip of her tongue drooped but Bridget's rose. And they touched. Moistened red tips I could see from the other side of the room where I stood rolling a cigarette or pouring a drink. And cleared my throat. Bridget turned to look me over and she laughed.

Don't be *nervous*, she said and I shook my head.

I wanted to say, who are you or I know who you are. But Ruth wouldn't understand. The Velvets played but I don't remember the music. After that I drank. Two wet flowers on the sofa, their slim limbs bound up in the other's and the tongues hidden and seen again. I didn't think anymore. Breathing like waves on driftwood or a seal carcass or the shore. Bridget flourished her wrists and laughed when Ruth's dress dropped, her hidden bare breasts now bared. Ruth didn't speak, touched her clavicle, touched her stiff brownish nipple.

She shrugged the dress from her elbows so it hung loose around her waist. She raised one hand to Bridget's face. Which took Bridget off guard, she pulled back slightly, but Ruth wouldn't stop. She touched Bridget's chin so soft with the thumb and came at her. It was the look that brought me to the couch, like I'd better intervene. Even their ankles were entangled. I stood quivering over them with my palms down like I would pet a wild thing.

Bridget looked up from the side of Ruth's jaw, who stood, her dress collapsed at her feet. She walked to the bottle and glass I'd left on the bookshelf, and poured herself a drink wearing a transparent kryptonite thong only. She looked up at me suddenly, and then at Bridget like she knew what I did not know. So it was that seed in her eye that caused me to take one last step but I didn't take another. Bridget on the couch with one breast bare. She covered it, and posed.

I didn't mean for you to feel left out, she said.

Ruth with a drink in her hand and she wasn't even watching. As if she didn't give a shit what I did. So maybe I'd been wrong about Ruth. She kept her eyes on Bridget like she'd rip the clothes from her body, fuck her, rip holes in her body. I turned back to Bridget who had partly risen with one hand up. I was looking at her face, an accusation. She would've taken me by the neck and brought me down to her but I pinned her with one hand. I could hear Ruth put down the glass when I grazed my tongue and teeth along Bridget's neck and she struggled to sit up again.

THIRTY-SEVEN

You'd picture us three in bed together sleeping with our ankles crossed. You'd imagine we'd wake up giggling and sheepish and James would bring us coffee or fruit juice with an eloquent label: pomegranate, cranberry, grape. And maybe then we'd have another go. But instead I lay in bed alone. James in his bag on the living room floor. Bridget naked on the couch, her thin arm over its arm, the pearly fingernails of her other hand scraping the floor. It was me who laid the blanket across her like she was dead.

I think it was their voices that woke me, my eyes swollen. They were whispering but I could still hear their voices although

I couldn't make out what they were saying in the living room, maybe nude still.

I wouldn't go in there. I wouldn't go in there ever until Bridget or James or I was dead, I thought. Or I would leave this apartment, this town, this valley. But I couldn't leave. I rubbed my face but I couldn't sit up, the weak light on my eyelids. My mouth dry, my throat sore. I thought I'd put a glass of water by the bed but when I looked there wasn't. Their whispers swelled, fell. I stood to a head spin and walked before I could see again. If they were sitting just so on the corner of the couch they would see my nude cross the hall from bedroom to bathroom but I didn't check. My piss a measly brown trickle. I drank from the tap, the water ticklish. I let the shower steam steep in the air before I stepped in.

When I'd finished they were still whispering.

So I got my face organized, lipstick, I dressed slowly. There wasn't a rush.

Soon enough I stood in the doorway.

James up close, talking in her ear, harsh, spittled, fast and lewd while she shook her head with her face hidden, her hair in a strange mat, a photograph in her hand. When James stopped to look up so she did too. His gun on the floor, the photographs scattered, some wrinkled old letters. She was ugly like I'd never seen her, her face wettish, reddish, her mascara streaked but she was proud, she'd won. She stood up like a wild thing, her tank top torn. She looked down at James, defiant when he grabbed her wrist.

Fuck you, she said and started toward me standing in the door.

Get back, James said.

I stepped back against the jamb, but he meant Bridget who shoved past me with James just behind. He didn't so much as glance at me. She pulled the door open and stumbled down the stairs. But he didn't follow, he turned with his eyes on the floor. He got his hands in his hair and rubbed his skull muttering something under his breath. Then he looked up, he looked up at me.

I thought maybe he'd hit me when he came at me fast. But he didn't. He put his arms around me, let all his weight down on me and let out a single screaming whine. It frightened me to watch an angry grown man sob even though we were just kids.

What, I said. What's happened.

When I looked back at the floor behind me, the gun was gone. But I didn't ask, I didn't care. Everything was empty but James spilling his sniveling, his tears. He clutched me, he held me tightly, tighter, squeezed the backs of my arms and my skin with his fingers. He gasped. He held me so tight that I gasped too, the smoke in the room now even with the windows shut and me trying to catch my breath while he cried and choked.

What, I said. What gives you the right.

I hated him. I fucking hated him. I folded my arms, then walked to the couch where last night at last I'd kissed Bridget's perfect tongue and lips, had my hands on her chest, and fucked her, or he had. The couch where they'd been whispering. I didn't want to sit, I didn't want him to say a thing.

It's not what you think, he said.

What makes you think you have any idea, *what* I think?

I didn't look at him.

You think, he said. It's Bridget I want. You know why? Because *you* want her, or you want to be her. Because you hate her.

I looked away. The shut windows above the couch were blank, were blankets of smoke. Everywhere was burning, I was burning. There was a cup of water on the coffee table. In a minute I would get it and drink. My face burned, my mind, my throat. I turned to look him in the eye.

It's crazy, he said.

I hated him. His slant-eyes just like Bridget's eyes. His perfect fucking mouth. I wouldn't hear another word. I would break. Something. He must've seen my look.

I'm trying to tell you, Ruth, he said.

I don't want to hear it, I screamed. I don't want to fucking hear it.

The coffee table took time to fall. But when it did the ashtray shattered and the ash and butts scattered. Paper lists caught the small low draft and flew across the floor. I regretted spilling the water.

God, I said.

Fine, he said. You don't want to listen, fucking fine.

He started out of the room, grabbed up his sleeping bag. I was on his heels.

I *thought* you were different, I said to the back of his head. Different than how everybody else goes for her over me, even me. Even. Me.

I covered my face with my hands but I knew he'd stopped. I was suffocating, choking on the smoke. He grabbed me by the skull and the roots of my hair so I had to look him in the face.

You're not listening, he said. You're not fucking listening. You're just freaking out. Just. Calm down. Fucking calm down. I mean, the way you're acting, it's. I *knew* you'd be this way. I *knew* you'd make a scene. Stop breathing like that. Stop it. *Stop* it.

He jerked my head back and I sobbed once, maybe it was in surprise. Maybe he was right, I didn't know anything but that he wanted Bridget. I could see in his bright bloodshot eyes that he hated me; I could smell his hot liquored breath, the stale smoke. My lips curled into a snarl. I was looking into *her* face, into Bridget's proud, gleaming black eyes. Fine.

I don't need to fucking calm down. All I need. Is for you. To get. Out. *Get* out.

I followed him into my bedroom where his pack was, cinched shut like he'd always been ready to make a run for it. I hoped he wouldn't; I wanted him to stay. To turn back and walk toward me, to take me by the nape and. He knelt and loosened the drawstring. Before he could start stuffing his sleeping bag in, I kicked the pack hard. It slid heavily across the floor toward the door. That's when I saw it. A small sack had slipped out with his t-shirts and toothbrush and opened, a wad of cash fallen from it. A wad of fifties.

I made it there before he did. I held the little sack to my chest; it was filled with cash. He started for me and I ran from the room. He owed me money. He should've been giving me money from the beginning. I was trying to get some bills loose, trying to think of where to go. The bathroom could be locked. So he'd have to break down the door. But I was already in the dark, stinking kitchen, looking frantically for somewhere to hide the money. I stuffed some bills under an empty booze bottle. The dishes piled in the sink, the trash full, the drawers hanging open. I turned fast when I heard him, a dull little knife in my hand and the sack at my back. He stood in the doorway, blocking the light so it burst from behind him, his face a black, blank mask although the gleam of his eyes was clear.

That's all you wanted, he said. All the time. Wasn't it. Wasn't it.

Which I could've just as well said to him.

You always knew. You knew I had it the whole time. They told you? They told you, you little.

Then he was up close, hissing in my face. The Evil Eye watching me, the barrel of the gun against me. He was. Delusional, worse than me. He didn't know what he was saying. I looked him in the eye with my chin up like I wasn't afraid. He snatched the money from my hand. But he hadn't gotten it all.

Get out, I said again.

I'm going, he said. I'm gone.

THIRTY-EIGHT

I had to find Bridget. Lose the pack, find her. I'd been walking and I was far from Ruth's place already. The smoky-hot, dry air, the pickup beds bumper-to-bumper all stacked high with mattresses and chairs, with televisions. Which meant evacuation. But I didn't care, I crossed at a diagonal, holding up my hands like a cop. And there I stood by my old digs the Bel Aire Motel. But I couldn't go inside. If I stashed my pack there it'd be too predictable and Ruth would know, they'd all know. I looked around and behind, and sure enough there was some blond bum I'd seen around, staggering and staring at the sidewalk like he didn't see me, like he wasn't on my trail. So I kept on.

I didn't know where she lived. I could hardly think of her name. Bridget. Good lips, good tits, and her half my sister. God, what was that supposed to mean? Nothing. And did I care? I would find her. I didn't know how much time had passed, I was smoking a cigarette on the corner by one drive-in bank or another. It was closed, even though it wasn't Sunday. An orange sign on the door but I didn't stop to read what it said. The traffic bad as Minneapolis rush hour. But the cars all packed like moving day. Daddy behind the wheel, and mom and the kids with terror in their eyes, staring out their shut windows at me like they all knew. Like they wanted my money and would get it. Then a cruiser, and the pig staring too. So I kept on. I had to get inside, hide. There was some kind of hotel there.

I was running; I was in the plush red lobby. But it was empty. Nobody at the bar, no little man at the piano, nobody behind the counter but one butch, bleached, and suited bitch saying, sir sir, there's no smoking in the hotel, sir, no smoking. She kept on talking saying, We recommend you follow instructions, evacuate. But I wasn't listening; I was trying to make out the river through the wall of windows behind her. It was close enough, but the smoke hid that.

Did it matter? With the cash, the gun, all I needed was a plan. I didn't know what I'd do. End Times Party tonight, already it was tonight. I didn't know where she lived, Bridget, but I could follow Ruth. Wait outside her place, keep my distance. Until Bridget's. The perfect hostess. Smiling with me and my pop's mouth, looking out from under my pop's eyebrows. And I'd walk right up. Step right up and.

THIRTY-NINE

I was pacing. I had my hair by the roots. In the end it was her. Bridget like always. James like everybody who chose her. Like every other girl or boy including me. So what had I expected if I knew I was shit, if I knew I was less than nothing. I was shit, I was trash, I was filth for wanting her too. I'd be better dead or gone. Dead and gone. Like the other Ruth, I'd be better off dead. I was already dead.

Bridget's mouth and her proud eyes. Whole and perfect, more than that. God I hated her. For taking James like I knew she would, for holding Lydia and Audrey over me, like I didn't already know I was expendable. For insulting me like I didn't notice. Like I was too drunk to care. She took everything from me. She didn't care about her so-soft lip in my teeth, my fingers in her hair while he was watching her only. Him standing with his eyes fixed on her. Just like I'd always known he would.

I was making a sound now, I could hear it in my throat, a groan choking me, gagging me, walking back and forth with him and her fucking in my face, in my mind and nothing else. I took a breath, flapping my hands like broken pigeon wings. I could leave. I could go anywhere but here. But that was just a lie; I was trapped, I didn't have a choice anymore. All flights from

Missoula were cancelled since yesterday already. Why hadn't I realized it'd gotten this bad? The smoke thick, worse than a blizzard. Maybe there were other ways. The Greyhound, the freights, hitching. Which disappointed me, that I still had hope. But I couldn't just wait, doing nothing. I had to stop this. Stop her him me.

Outside was hell. The Rattlesnake fire had been rolling down toward town, the smoke pouring into the valley thick as shit. My eyes on fire and me choking, coughing. I couldn't stand it out there, I couldn't stay outside for one second longer but there was nowhere to go. Maybe I didn't care, maybe I'd done it on purpose. I'd never leave now. Evacuation was for yuppies. Evacuation was for assholes dumb enough to think there was a way out.

So maybe I was only out there looking for James even though I wouldn't find him. I walked this way and turned and walked away and back. I couldn't think with my mind on fire, with the whole fucking world on fire I couldn't see a thing. I had my hand in my purse and money in my hand. It was seven bills I'd hid, fifties. If things were different, I might've saved it for rent, for a ticket out, for the party. If I didn't have enough for the party, they'd probably kick me out. But instead I was in the pawnshop before I knew it, my hands on the case, my eyes on the bloated diamonds inside. And from the back there appeared a slick little man, wiping his hands. His eyes red, his teeth so white.

Engaged, miss? he said. Despite the circumstances, my congratulations. Celebration in this difficulty. It's just what is wanted. Yes, I believe I have just the one.

From behind the case he slid open the glass and reached for one haughty chunk of chintz, his fingernails perfectly mani-cured. The rifles hung behind him, the pistols locked in the next case. I held up my hand.

What I came for, I said. What I came for is a gun.

I had the bills out. They didn't mean anything—just little

paper scraps. His eyes flicked up at me. He must've seen the money already, from the moment I walked through the door. His hand frozen above a clump of measly diamonds. The lubricated skin around his mouth stretched. I didn't smile back.

Yes, said the little man. That's something else entirely. You know our policy, there's a twenty-four-hour waiting period of course.

Have you been outside? The valley is *on fire*. And there's all these militants with tens of thousands of rounds of ammunition stockpiled, and then there's me. Just a girl, all alone.

Maybe it was true, maybe that was how it looked from the outside. His eyes fixed on me, his lips tight together, his ten fingers pressed so hard against the glass case that his knuckles went white. But when I looked around I could see the moving boxes stacked in the corner of the store. Besides the gun racks, the shelves were mostly empty. He was packing up for good.

It's a legal issue, he said. I could lose my license if I sell some pretty little thing a gun she don't know how to use and she up and kills somebody.

By tomorrow Missoula's going to burn. And you're going to be a thousand miles from here. Nobody'll even know what all you brought with you. For all they know this whole place went up in smoke.

Maybe I believed what I was saying. Maybe I didn't. He stared blankly at me for a long time. But then, in one quick move, he took out a little pistol and set it on the glass top of the case.

That's all well and good, miss. And I'll sell it to you, given the circumstances. But I regret to inform you, you can't shoot wildfire.

FORTY

By dusk I was calm, my mind a blank. I hadn't opened my invitation. I'd been practicing in the mirror—to my temple, or with my teeth tight around the barrel, or pointed at my reflection. 38 Special pointed at me and not me.

I didn't know when I was expected, but I was walking north toward Bridget's. Even Worden's was closed, with a little sign that read: Stay Alive! And every car or truck that passed was loaded down like they were leaving for good. On the block of houses that'd been re-zoned commercial—the law offices, the accountants, the chiropractors—there were a couple of men in official-looking hazmat suits spraying flame-retardant gel on the walls, on the roofs, on the windows. But in the end it didn't look much different than before. Breathing was hell so I walked slow, I didn't see the point in going quickly now. Someone was watching. I glanced behind but didn't see much besides parked cars and one old long-haired bum leaning his head on his shopping cart.

Bridget's was the only lit house on the block. For an evacuation, it was strange how many people were inside. I lit a cigarette standing on the sidewalk watching the faceless bodies silhouetted in the red-curtained windows. Next door, her neighbors had boarded up the windows, as if that would help.

The door hung open. I put my hand in my purse and held the cool steel. I hadn't shot it yet, but the little man showed me what to do. There were many cars parked along the block, shadowed and glinting beneath the streetlights. Pickups like always, and the black Hummer again, at the end of the block. Inside fast, fat music started, and the voices matched it. The black Hummer again. I stubbed out my cigarette all but unsmoked.

Nobody was watching the door, so I shut it behind me, to try and keep the smoke out. Her place didn't look the same, but it took me a minute to realize she'd painted the walls black.

Only up close did I see there were words written everywhere, in black too. Across the walls randomly. I leaned close to read. It was a joke, it was the graffiti from the party house. No Outside Nothing but outside. I die.

The living room was thick with bodies, a bowl of red punch on the coffee table in the middle. I didn't see any randoms, everyone there was a veteran. Everybody was drinking from red cups, and the punch had stained their lips and teeth, like vampires but afraid. Nobody had dressed up, everyone was dressed in leather or wife beaters and combat boots like Arnold or Sarah Connor in prison. I'll be back. I knew all their faces. If I tried I could distinguish each one from the others even though they all looked the same. They chewed dully with their bloodshot eyes and foreheads glistening. The light was too bright, vibrating florescent. And they were specimens beneath it, packed so tight you couldn't really dance.

It was too cold inside, but nobody else seemed to care. And the smell was wrong, like something had died in the walls, like air freshener. Bridget stood to one side laughing, Lydia was talking, Audrey scanned the room. When she saw me, she leaned to whisper one syllable in Lydia's ear. Lydia in black, Audrey in gunmetal without makeup. I turned away.

I needed a drink so I went to the kitchen which was empty except for one rough kid whose name I forgot. The kitchen was the same as ever, all the knives neatly magnetized on the wall. The kid was drunk, leaning against the counter smiling, spilling red punch from his cup. She'd never set the oven clock and it flashed red 12:21, 12:21, 12:21. It looked like most of the liquor was in the punch but there was a half-empty bottle of tequila and a bottle of Red Apple Liqueur with a bright splash at the bottom.

The fucking world's coming to an end, he said. But you got to have a drink.

I poured tequila on ice and turned to go.

Punch's in the other room, he slurred. Drinks in the other room.

He leered.

Punch makes you fat, I said.

I know you, he said. I've seen you.

I drank. You know some girl died at the last party. Ruth. She's dead.

He started to laugh. Who fucking cares. The cops don't. They probably all left. Poof. With everybody else.

His eyes huge and bright; it was more than booze. I wondered what they were selling tonight. Something new. I put my hand in my purse. I couldn't think of what I was supposed to say. I wouldn't cry; I wouldn't do a thing.

In the living room, Marilyn Monroe hung in a broken, glassless frame. Bridget with a bottle of tequila, dressed in kelly-green and her hair loose at the top of her head. Pathetic, the only one all dressed up like nobody'd told her the theme was *Terminator.* But then again, this wasn't really her party. They were just using her. A business major she'd been sleeping with for a little while stood just behind her pretending to look bored but his eyes were bright and frightened. His knuckles white, he was holding a red net bag of limes and a knife.

Hey, I said to Bridget.

I didn't look at Lydia or Audrey. But Bridget didn't say anything; she was staring hard, just over my shoulder. She took a step back and reached out her hand, as if the business major would do something for her. But he was trying to dance, pumping his hips, looking back and forth and swallowing, his adam's apple dove and resurfaced, dove and resurfaced. His hands above his head like a stickup, the red net bag swinging slowly with the music. When I turned it was James she'd been watching, striding through the vibrating bodies with his eyes on her like if there was an exit she was it.

We need to talk, he said.

Talk? she said and looked him up and down.

She laughed and didn't look at Lydia or Audrey.

Yeah, talk, he said. You owe me that.

God, she said and laughed. What an embarrassing thing to say.

Look I came to *Montana*. The least you can do is.

She shrugged. I had my hand in my purse, one finger on the trigger. I touched his shoulder and he glanced at me, but turned back to Bridget. I was very cold. I wrapped my arm around my stomach.

We need to *talk*, James said again.

Audrey turned to me.

Bridget told us you were feeling left *out* the other night.

God don't look so serious, Bridget said to James. You look so *serious*.

Serious? Have you *been* outside? But the point is. *A lone*.

Audrey had her head cocked and her brow in a knit. She was pretending to care. Lydia was looking at something behind me. Or someone. She frowned.

Finally, Lydia said. Crystal's here. Excuse me.

She stepped around me.

I mean, Audrey said. We thought it was totally weird how you just *bounced*. But Bridget said you felt bad like she was moving on. You shouldn't feel *bad*.

What? I said.

I could take her with me, I was thinking.

I mean, this is why I came here, James said. I mean. I came all the way to fucking *Montana*. And I'm not going to *leave* until you. Tell me. Until you. Tell me.

But he couldn't come up with what it was he wanted from her. It would've been so easy to press the mouth of the barrel to Audrey's smooth forehead and... But Audrey didn't matter. She glanced behind me, at Lydia and Crystal, probably making a deal. Bridget watched too.

Bridget, James said. *Bridget.*

God, she said, looking back at him. Okay you want to be *alone?* Take the bottle.

She jammed it at his chest and turned to walk away as if she would take him to her bedroom. This was it. I couldn't let them leave. Not to her bedroom, in front of me just like that. I took the gun out fast and cocked it the way the little man had done and pressed it to my temple like this was a movie.

Oh, Audrey said. My *God.*

Audrey's voice rose.

Bridget, she said.

Bridget turned. And James pulled his own gun out, gut reaction. Made mine look pretty and light; his was big enough to break you in two. Nobody noticed but me.

Oh, she said. That's not *funny,* Ruth. Put it down. Put it *down.*

I laughed. His gun wouldn't make a difference now. They were both looking at me. At last they were looking at me; they saw me and not each other. Their eyebrows up, their hands rising with the palms to the floor. I paused, and smiled at James who glanced at Bridget without moving his head. He took a step toward me. What was he going to do, shoot me? I laughed and took a step back.

Ruth, he said. Put it down, babe. It's okay, I'll take it. Give it to me. You can give it to me.

He held out his hand.

Babe? I said. Seems like that'd be Bridget.

I pointed it at him, walking slowly backward and laughed. I didn't feel anything really, I was watching from the outside, this was just another thing happening.

It's not *funny,* Bridget said again.

The cops aren't going to come, I told her. The cops are *gone.*

I don't know why I said that. Like a threat? Everybody was watching. The room was still except for breathing. Everybody watched. Bridget and James. Audrey. Lydia and Crystal against the wall at a distance with money in their hands. But the baby wasn't there. Crystal but no baby; it was probably dead.

I should've been more careful. I shouldn't have stumbled.

I'd let myself get distracted and I stumbled backward and reached around to get my balance back. James was on me, bent my fingers the wrong direction and wrenched the gun from my hand. The bowl of punch slid across the coffee table, fell and shattered in splinters of glass like a scream. Red liquid everywhere as if it was blood, as if it had already happened. I didn't fall but he'd gotten it, the gun was gone. The music played and everybody stared but I didn't look up. I had my eyes on the ground while he shook the butt of it in my face. I was pathetic. I was nothing, I was shit. Fire, I thought, Fire.

You have no fucking *business* with a gun, he said. What made you think you could have a gun? You don't know what to do with a gun. You don't have a fucking clue.

He had it in both hands, his fingers working, fumbling. It was so much littler than his. His long fingers ungainly like pubescent boys trying for a fuck. I was calm now, watching him like this was usual, like I was in charge, like I hadn't just humiliated myself in front of everyone. My smile was bitter and tight. But he wasn't looking, he was swearing, I guess he was trying to lower the hammer. Turned the gun over, his fingers, fingers. Around him guests drank again, and glanced at each other disappointed that the End of the World Party wasn't a better show.

Give it back. I'll *do* it. Let me. It's mine. It's *mine*.

My palm hovered just above the metal when it fired.

Everybody was screaming. James screamed without sound, his eyes and rictus wide, soft inside. The gun dropped. I knelt to pick it up before I saw Bridget slumped on the floor, red as punch, thick blood filled her midriff and her perfect tits till I couldn't see them anymore. Was this what I'd really wanted? My stomach gone, my cold skin wet. Her lids fluttered. But she was breathing. Her blood red rose, fell. James turned to me.

You killed her, he said. You. You killed her.

I took a step back. 38 Special. I had my gun again. I could shoot me now. If I wanted to. It would be quick. I knew what to do. Bridget on the floor. The smell.

But I didn't, I said.

He pointed at the gun in my hand.

Yes, you did, he said. You killed her. *You* killed her.

What?

He came at me, standing over me panting, rubbing at his skull with his fingers, pulling at his hair, his jaw clenched, loathing me. Loathing me.

You fucking crazy bitch you fucking crazy delusional you can't even see what's in front of you. I've been telling you but you can't even fucking see and now you killed her you killed her. And she's my sister she's my fucking sister but you wouldn't stop long enough to let me say it you could only see that I wanted her but it was *you*. Because *you* did and now she's *dead*.

I thought he would hit me, or shoot me, but he didn't. He stepped away from me and dropped his head, his hands on his knees like he was going to throw up. I looked at Bridget, who slit her eyes and mouthed something I couldn't make out. Audrey bent down with her phone in her hand.

But she's not, I said. I didn't.

Your *sister*? Lydia said. God. What a joke.

I have to call the police, Audrey said. I have to call 911.

Nobody laughed. James stood up.

You better get out of here, Ruth, James said. You better run. You don't know the cops are gone. They could be here, right now, outside the door right now.

Audrey stood up and stepped toward him, her hands shaking.

You're the one, she said to him. I saw you. It was *you*. It was *you*.

The swarm of eyes on him. The red lips still, the red cups. I stepped back, away from him. He looked down at Bridget and his face contorted. James fell on his knees. Started rubbing at his skull, started pulling at his hair. My heart in my gullet and Bridget with her eyelids smooth. Her chest rose and fell but he didn't see.

She's dead, he said. Oh God. God. It's. She's dead.

He grabbed my wrist hard and snatched me close. He shoved me toward the door and I struggled against him. He got his other hand on the back of my neck and pushed me forward through the stares.

Nobody tried to stop us.

I choked when we stepped outside. There was no air left, only smoke, and no car passed, no cruiser with its lights and sirens going. The rumble of an idling pickup was the only sound from the black still street. We paused. It was an old blue Ford with the cab's dome light on but nobody inside. Crystal's truck. James had his hand on the small of my back and he pushed me toward it. He must've forgotten about my gun. I brushed the back of his hand with the barrel but he didn't notice. Or I could shoot him. Right. Now.

Get in, he said. Get in. Get in the *fucking* truck.

He opened the door and I slid across the slick vinyl bench to the passenger's. Through the smoke it smelled like something soft, something I couldn't identify. I looked down at my hands, 38 Special nice and light. He slammed the door.

He grabbed it from me and shoved it underneath his seat. My one shot gone.

You're taking Crystal's truck, I said.

He didn't look at me, slammed it into drive and gassed it.

FORTY-ONE

Someone is watching us, I was thinking. Someone planned it like this.

The radio at full blast. James drove fast on the freeway east, cursing, beating the wheel. We curved through Hellgate, the two hills ascending dimly on either side, the black trees, the river. It was hidden by condominiums and appeared again glowing dully red in the light from someplace.

I know you stole from me, he said. What, you thought I wouldn't notice? How much did you take? You thought I wouldn't care? You thought I wouldn't get it back?

I had my hand on my chest. My heart in my throat, in my belly, in my throat, in my third eye, in his Evil Eye but I felt nothing. I got out a crumpled cigarette from the pack on the dash and lit it. We were driving somewhere in the dark like a getaway, but there wasn't any escape. Bridget wasn't dead. She couldn't be dead, would never be. She'd been breathing but anyway she would've found a way to carry on. The train appeared, entering the valley from the opposite direction. Its bodiless spotlight fell on us and James raised his hand to shield his eyes, pale and glistening.

What is it? he was screaming. What is it? What is it?

I turned the radio down.

The train, I said and laughed. What. You thought the cops had come?

A sound, a little grunt from the backseat made us both turn. I don't know why we hadn't looked before, or realized. Crystal's baby. Crystal's fucking baby. It tried to sit up, to see over its shoulder. But it was strapped in so it gave up and lifted one puny hand and let it drop. James watched in the rear-view with his knuckles white on the wheel.

I was on my knees facing backward. I couldn't look away but it didn't try and look back. I'd been wrong about it when I'd left it for dead with Ruth. Because now it'd returned, my tiny executioner. I should've killed it when I had the chance. I could smell it stronger now that I'd seen it there in the dark. It wasn't the real thing, but at least I could see it, dressed like before in a filthy blue suit. It wanted me to answer, but I wouldn't.

I sat back down hard when James slammed on the brakes. Through the windshield red lights were flashing. At first I didn't see it was a sign.

Fire Incident Ahead, it read. Highway 90 East closed.

Which meant we were trapped. There were cruisers in the shoulder with their lights flashing, cops in the road in reflective vests, kryptonite and orange. A line-up of old campers, shit-box pickups, and busted station wagons—the last of the evacuees—and cops pacing, shining their flashlights through vehicle windows.

Exit, I screamed. Exit exit exit.

We were at Bonner, and he jerked the wheel to the right so sudden that cop heads popped up. They'd seen us. The huge truck stop before us, florescents and semis' high beams illuminating the smoke and it, beneath the invisible, dark mountains. We'd stopped at an intersection. James was beating at the wheel but for a moment I didn't speak, I couldn't feel my body.

Turn right, I said. Go right go right we'll take Deer Creek Road up over.

Over? Over *where*? There's nowhere, God they're going to kill me. God God.

I could see the cops on the freeway, and the evacuees. One cruiser was driving the wrong way toward the exit. I hadn't heard about any fires in the Sapphires, but that was yesterday. I got up on my knees and grabbed James by the face.

Think, I said through my teeth. There's a cop coming right now. *Right* now. We'll. Go into the Sapphires. Fucking *drive*.

He slammed on the gas and I barely caught myself on the dash.

It wasn't me talking, it was the animal talking self-preservation.

I didn't care if I was caught or not, I was dead anyway. And yet, when the police found us, I'd say I'd been kidnapped. I'd take care of the baby, and they'd believe me. Even cops liked kids.

She's dead, he said and looked up. She's dead. She's dead. She's dead.

We were on gravel now, driving up into the mountains, larch branches grazing the windows. I was getting tossed around the cab since Deer Creek was just a glorified logging road, all rutted out, winding up the backside of Hellgate and into the Sapphires, all the way south to Hamilton.

She's dead, he said. She's dead. She's dead.

Stop it, I said. Stop it. She's not fucking *dead*. It's just. She can't be.

It was just to get him to shut up.

Just shut up, I said. Just shut up.

But he didn't stop until there were headlights behind us, back down the switchback. Low down lights, like a sedan's. Like a cruiser's. We didn't say anything but he gassed it, the bed fishtailing, his hands tight and loose and tight on the wheel. I squeezed my eyes shut to try and keep my head from jostling off. Until he made a wrenching, whining groan.

We're running out of gas, he hissed. I cannot fucking believe this. We're running out of fucking gas.

FORTY-TWO

He'd pulled off into the trees and the truck rolled downhill until it died, just barely out of sight of the road. I ran back uphill and lay flat to the ground to watch. I didn't have to wait long. But we were well-enough out of sight for him to miss us. At least for now. If they were really looking, it wouldn't take long. Close to the ground the smoke was lighter, the air cool and sweet with broken pine needles. I lay my head down. I was very tired. I was exhausted. I couldn't keep my eyes open.

I started to dream right away, of a ship but I don't know how long I slept. When I woke I could've made a run for it but I started back to the truck. James was gone but the baby was there in the back seat, awake but silent. I didn't touch it. It was filthy, strapped down in its little plastic prison.

It didn't thrust its little hands into the air; it hardly made a sound. I was supposed to find it some milk or something. I let the truck door swing open and stepped out again where behind the smoke it must've been dawn. I circled the truck, but James was nowhere. There were only stumps and stunted trees on every side. And a path downhill.

Maybe somebody would come and take the kid away. I started downhill and soon I was on state land that hadn't been logged in years. Just slim trees shadowed bluish in the smoky light and the ash sky falling on me, the smoke. It should've been silent, but the highway pulsed hoarsely from below. I listened, the smoke thickened.

The little trail leveled and I stood at the edge of a clearing.

I saw it right away: a tree house. And James, crouched in the tall grass before it with his gun in his hand as if he would use it. I hadn't expected it to be that easy in the end. There was a breeze that moved the grasses and the treetops around the tree house. Its floor was made of whole, fresh logs lashed together, its roof just twisted branches. The walls were filthy plywood, three cut-out windows covered in frosted plastic. A rope ladder hung down swinging. It was just some bum's elevated shack but I was transfixed.

I suppose I heard the helicopter, but I didn't duck until it was directly overhead. Like I thought it was coming for us. But it had a full red water tank hanging. And it was going south, which meant there was a new fire, somewhere close in the Sapphires. It was then the smoke, bloated and black, billowed sails from over the top of the hill. The helicopter disappeared into it. I must've been breathing.

James hadn't seen. He slowly raised his hand hello. Slowly I raised my hand.

If I could've turned back, I'd forgotten.

FORTY-THREE

I didn't wait for Ruth. I didn't see the tree house until I was under it, the rope ladder swinging in the predawn. I watched the tree house gather smoky light until here came Wilbur's legs through the trap-door in the floor, and he climbed slowly down with a rifle over his shoulder. I can't say I'd known it would be him, but I wasn't surprised. First three rules: you could die, you could die, don't get caught. I was very tired. I sat, the grasses high as my chin.

He jumped from the bottom rung and watched me stand but didn't say a thing. Agile for an old timer, for a dying man if he was. He didn't say, Come on in then. And he didn't say, Well all right I figured you'd make it up this way. Or, Get. Or, You ain't welcome here. He just stood with his arms crossed and leaned against the trunk of one of the trees his place was built on.

Paris, he said. Put the gun down.

I looked down at it, in my hand. I'd forgotten. And let it drop, I wouldn't touch it anymore forever. It lay, dull in the grass like nothing for killing.

I'm not him, I said. My father is dead.

Ruth stood beside me now, she had been there for a while already with her mascara smudged, her skin sallow and slack and gleaming. I hated her. I took her hand. Maybe it was for this, the having some girl's hand to take, having some girl standing just behind you that kept the whole thing shuffling along. The grasses susurrated in a sudden smoky breeze. Crows above us, hung from greasy black wings. Wilbur didn't come any closer.

What, so you left her for dead? I told you it would come to that. Didn't I tell you?

She's *not* dead, I said.

From the first I knew you was no account. All these years I done right by you. Never said a word against you. But this. To try and kill a woman you profess to love. The woman you could not keep your hands off and you a married man.

I let go of Ruth's hand.

I don't know what you're talking about, I said. It wasn't my fault. It was her. Her.

It's a sin. *Adultery.* A sin. *Murder.* A sin.

It was *her* gun, I said.

But Ruth wasn't listening. She stood facing away from me at an angle, watching.

What's next, *incest*, he said. It's inhuman, inhuman.

I only wanted, I said. To lower the hammer. I only wanted. I didn't know, I didn't.

But I didn't go on because he lifted the rifle and aimed, clicked the safety off and found me in the eye of the scope. I held up my hands and stepped back, I didn't deserve to die. I had to use the bathroom, had to, I couldn't wait anymore. I'd been shaking my head, my hands and legs weak. My insides nothing, my mind. I didn't deserve to die.

Legs through the trap-door. And his woman came slowly down the ladder. She had their perfect baby on her back, her long skirt swinging. Wilbur didn't look up from through the eye of the scope when she jumped in a little burst of dust. I don't know how long I'd known, but I couldn't pretend not to see anymore: the fire was here. Billows of smoke poured from over the hillside behind her.

Walk, he said. Walk.

I didn't move. I couldn't move. For a time I didn't know what walk was. I had to keep thinking, One foot before the other. I didn't want to die. The smoke poured blackish downhill. His woman turned to watch. The baby didn't cry, it didn't make a sound.

Get, he said. Move. You know I don't care for repeating myself.

I turned. Ruth had taken a few steps and stopped. She had her hand over her face. Her eyes black milk, her eyes black smoke reflecting. And Wilbur with his rifle. Maybe he wouldn't do it, maybe if we did what he told us he'd let me go. Or I could make a run for it. I could run into the trees and the smoke would hide me and I'd escape.

Ruth started to walk and I followed heavily. Ruth gasping, her breath rasping. She slowed until I caught up to her, her shoulders slouched and her forehead glistening. I didn't breathe, could smell my skull and Ruth, the stink of liquor coming off her and smoke. I stopped but Wilbur was close behind, the grass to his nipples, the rifle as long as him, little man. But laughing only made me fall on my knees and he was on me, the cold barrel tucked up under the back of my skull. I had my hands up, I got up.

Something funny? he said.

To which I shook my head. But he hit me hard in the mouth with the butt of the gun. I came to with my face in the grass and the dry ground. There was air down there; I gasped. The road far above me, and I could see the truck's wheels when I lifted my eyes.

Get up, Wibur said.

At the truck Ruth stood with her arms slack by her sides.

It's gone, she said. The kid's gone. Somebody must've. Taken it.

The car seat empty, all the doors hung open. And smoke and smoke.

Wilbur's woman was gone. Ruth pointed her finger at me.

He made me go with him, she said. Forced me.

Paris, he said. Forced? Edith? Your own wife? Edith who we love?

Edith is my mother's name, I said.

But I was talking to myself. Wilbur's lifted brow, wild half-smile at Ruth who was pale and sunk-eyed, slouching more and more like somebody was drinking her from within. I didn't smile anymore, it was so difficult now. Ruth ran her fingers through her hair, her face a twist, her chest falling and falling—there wasn't any air. I'd wanted to make a run for it, but what I needed was water and I looked at Ruth like I'd find it there.

She was slow as hell, so I got her by the wrist. I didn't know where we were, nowhere, there was no way out. The smoke over the hillcrest. Black in my eyes, in my chest, in my throat choking. Spots of nothing in my gaze and one of them big as a man or woman silhouette standing on the hilltop there. Him or her all black in the smoke, turning to look back down at me walking uphill so slow below. The little man didn't seem to see; he swung his arms holding his gun stiff and then he stopped and aimed again right at me.

So I tried to run dropping footfalls like shits on the hill, my eyes on that woman or man silhouette upon it. The hill must've kept on but in the smoke I didn't see. I was blind and Ruth was gone. I walked alone. If I went a little faster, I might escape, I might catch him or her in the smoke there looking back at me, little nothing, always looking back looking back again. If I ran I would catch up I would catch up if I ran. I stopped to gasp. His or her silhouette low on the rocks there. And if I squinted I could see that face like mine, lifted chin, slant eyes, black hair.

The hill was nearly ended. It might've been the first one we'd climbed or another. We'd gone so far already, I didn't know how much time had passed. Sweat and smoke in my eyes and spittle in the open crack of my open mouth but I couldn't breathe I ran. I was not thinking, I was apart and I stood where that other man or woman had, in the rocks. I dreamed a dry valley falling from me. And a finger's width away were wild red horses. Were thick black horses.

There was no man or woman, there was nothing but those many vast black dumb thick eyes watching as if there was such a thing as human feeling, as if there was such a thing as understanding. Muscles and necks and skulls flung back with the mane knotted up for the sky and their snorting deafening. I covered my ears; I fell on my knees. One stamped and another and another and another to trample me and I die. The ground ruptured and the black shit trees falling in the red and the black so close I could watch their breath unfurling flame from soft lewd nostrils while they bared blunt teeth and eyeballs and skulls so close surrounding us watching us fall again and again and again.

FREQUENCIES

A new non-fiction journal of artful essays.

"The quality of each piece makes this journal heavy with literary weight."
—*NewPages*

VOLUME 1 / FALL 2012

Essays by Blake Butler, Joshua Cohen, Tracy Rose Keaton, Scott McClanahan; Interview with Anne Carson.

VOLUME 2 / SPRING 2013

Essays by Sara Finnerty, Roxane Gay, Alex Jung, Aaron Shulman, Kate Zambreno; A discussion about ghosts featuring Mark Z. Danielewski, Grace Krilanovich, Douglas Coupland, and others; Plus, T. S. Eliot interviews T. S. Eliot!

VOLUME 3 / FALL 2013

Lawrence Shainberg travels with George Plimpton and Norman Mailer to Vienna; D. Foy on the ko-opting of Krump; Antonia Crane on blue collar work; Andrew Miller avoids his soft cell; and Eric Obenauf on birthday presents during the Great Recession!

A QUESTIONABLE SHAPE
A NOVEL BY BENNETT SIMS

"[*A Questionable Shape*] is more than just a novel. It is literature. It is life."
—*The Millions*

"Presents the yang to the yin of Whitehead's *Zone One*, with chess games, a dinner invitation, and even a romantic excursion. Echoes of [Thomas] Bernhard's hammering circularity and [David Foster] Wallace's bright mind that can't stop making connections are both present. The point is where the mind goes, and, in that respect, Sims has his thematic territory down cold." —*The Daily Beast*

CRAPALACHIA
A NOVEL BY SCOTT MCCLANAHAN

"[McClanahan] aims to lasso the moon… He is not a writer of half-measures. The man has purpose. This is his symphony, every note designed to resonate, to linger." —*New York Times Book Review*

"*Crapalachia* is the genuine article: intelligent, atmospheric, raucously funny and utterly wrenching. McClanahan joins Daniel Woodrell and Tom Franklin as a master chronicler of backwoods rural America." —*The Washington Post*

MIRA CORPORA
A NOVEL BY JEFF JACKSON

"Eerie and enigmatic debut. The prose works like the expressionless masks worn by killers in horror films." —*Wall Street Journal*

"A gutter punk *Catcher in the Rye*."
—*Shelf Awareness*

SEVEN DAYS IN RIO
A NOVEL BY FRANCIS LEVY

"The funniest American novel since Sam Lipsyte's *The Ask*."
—*Village Voice*

"Like an erotic version of Luis Bunuel's *The Discreet Charm of the Bourgeoisie*."
—*The Cult*

THE SHANGHAI GESTURE
A NOVEL BY GARY INDIANA

"An uproarious, confounding, turbocharged fantasia that manages, alongside all its imaginative bravura, to hold up to our globalized epoch the fun-house mirror it deserves." —*Bookforum*

THE OTHER SIDE OF THE WORLD
A NOVEL BY JAY NEUGEBOREN

"Epic... *The Other Side of the World* can charm you with its grace, intelligence and scope... [An] inventive novel." —*The Washington Post*

"Neugeboren presents a meditation on life, love, art and family relationships that's reminiscent of the best of John Updike." —*Kirkus Reviews*

THE CAVE MAN
A NOVEL BY XIAODA XIAO

* *WOSU* (NPR member station) Favorite Book of 2009.

"As a parable of modern China, [*The Cave Man*] is chilling." —*Boston Globe*

SOME THINGS THAT MEANT THE WORLD TO ME
A NOVEL BY JOSHUA MOHR

* *O, The Oprah Magazine* '10 Terrific Reads of 2009.'

"Charles Bukowski fans will dig the grit in this seedy novel, a poetic rendering of postmodern San Francisco." —*O, The Oprah Magazine*

BABY GEISHA
STORIES BY TRINIE DALTON

"[The stories] feel like brilliant sexual fairy tales on drugs. Dalton writes of self-discovery and sex with a knowing humility and humor." —*Interview Magazine*

HOW TO GET INTO THE TWIN PALMS
A NOVEL BY KAROLINA WACLAWIAK

"One of my favorite books this year." —*The Rumpus*

"Waclawiak's novel reinvents the immigration story."
—*New York Times Book Review*, Editors' Choice

RADIO IRIS
A NOVEL BY ANNE-MARIE KINNEY

"Kinney is a Southern California Camus." —*Los Angeles Magazine*

"[*Radio Iris*] has a dramatic otherworldly payoff that is
unexpected and triumphant." —*New York Times Book Review*,
Editors' Choice

THE PEOPLE WHO WATCHED HER PASS BY
A NOVEL BY SCOTT BRADFIELD

"Challenging [and] original... A billowy adventure of a book. In
a book that supplies few answers, Bradfield's lavish eloquence is
the presiding constant." —*New York Times Book Review*

I'M TRYING TO REACH YOU
A NOVEL BY BARBARA BROWNING

✱ *The Believer* Book Award Finalist.

"I think I love this book so much because it contains intimations
of the potential of what books can be in the future, and also
because it's hilarious." —Emily Gould, *BuzzFeed*

THE ORANGE EATS CREEPS
A NOVEL BY GRACE KRILANOVICH

✱ National Book Foundation 2010 '5 Under 35' Selection.
✱ NPR Best Books of 2010.
✱ *The Believer* Book Award Finalist.

"Krilanovich's work will make you believe that new ways of
storytelling are still emerging from the margins." —*NPR*

NOG
A NOVEL BY RUDOLPH WURLITZER

"[*Nog*'s] combo of Samuel Beckett syntax and hippie-era freakiness mapped out new literary territory for generations to come."
—*Time Out New York*

THE DROP EDGE OF YONDER
A NOVEL BY RUDOLPH WURLITZER

✱ *Time Out New York*'s Best Book of 2008.
✱ *ForeWord* Magazine 2008 Gold Medal in Literary Fiction.
"A picaresque American *Book of the Dead*… in the tradition of Thomas Pynchon, Joseph Heller, Kurt Vonnegut, and Terry Southern." —*Los Angeles Times*

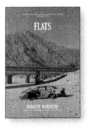

FLATS / QUAKE
TWO CLASSIC NOVELS BY RUDOLPH WURLITZER

"Wurlitzer might be the closest thing we have to an actual cult author, a highly talented fiction writer."
—*Barnes & Noble Review*

"Together they provide a tour of the dissolution of identity that was daily life in the sixties."
—Michael Silverblatt, *KCRW's Bookworm*

DAMASCUS
A NOVEL BY JOSHUA MOHR

"*Damascus* succeeds in conveying a big-hearted vision."
—*The Wall Street Journal*

"Nails the atmosphere of a San Francisco still breathing in the smoke that lingers from the days of Jim Jones and Dan White." —*New York Times Book Review*

1940
A NOVEL BY JAY NEUGEBOREN

✱ Long list, 2010 International IMPAC Dublin Literary Award.

"Intelligent and absorbing… subtle and affecting."
—*Washington Post*

"Jay Neugeboren traverses the Hitlerian tightrope with all the skill and formal daring that have made him one of our most honored writers of literary fiction and masterful nonfiction."
—*Los Angeles Times*

TERMITE PARADE
A NOVEL BY JOSHUA MOHR

✱ *Sacramento Bee* Best Read of 2010.

"[A] wry and unnerving story of bad love gone rotten. [Mohr] has a generous understanding of his characters, whom he describes with an intelligence and sensitivity that pulls you in. This is no small achievement." —*New York Times Book Review*

I SMILE BACK
A NOVEL BY AMY KOPPELMAN

"Powerful. Koppelman's instincts help her navigate these choppy waters with inventiveness and integrity." —*Los Angeles Times*

EROTOMANIA: A ROMANCE
A NOVEL BY FRANCIS LEVY

✱ *Queerty* Top 10 Book of 2008.
✱ *Inland Empire Weekly* Standout Book of 2008.

"Miller, Lawrence, and Genet stop by like proud ancestors."
—*Village Voice*